SOY SAUCE FOR BEGINNERS

SOY SAUCE
FOR
BEGINNERS

KIRSTIN CHEN

New Harvest
Houghton Mifflin Harcourt
BOSTON   NEW YORK
2014

For information about permission to reproduce selections from this book,
write to Permissions, Houghton Mifflin Harcourt Publishing Company,
215 Park Avenue South, New York, New York 10003.

www.hmhco.com

Library of Congress Cataloging-in-Publication Data
Chen, Kirsten.
Soy sauce for beginners / Kirsten Chen.
pages cm
ISBN 978-0-544-11439-5 (hardback)
1. Asian American women — Fiction. 2. Americans — Singapore — Fiction.
3. Family-owned business enterprises — Fiction. 4. Soy sauce industry — Fiction.
5. Domestic fiction. I. Title.
PS3603.H4495S69 2013
813'.6 — dc23
2013010179

Printed in the United States of America
DOC 10 9 8 7 6 5 4 3 2 1

Soy Sauce for Beginners

1

THESE ARE SOME OF MY FAVORITE smells: toasting bagel, freshly cut figs, the bergamot in good Earl Grey tea, a jar of whole soybeans slowly turning beneath a tropical sun.

You'd expect the latter to smell salty, meaty, flaccid — like what you'd smell if you unscrewed the red cap of the bottle on a table in your neighborhood Chinese restaurant and stuck your nose in as far as it would go. But real, fermenting soybeans smell nothing like sauce in a plastic bottle. Tangy and pungent, like rising bread or wet earth, these soybeans smell of history, of life, of tiny, patient movements, unseen by the naked eye.

Everything I know about soy sauce I learned from my father and my uncle and my late grandfather. We are a family who can talk endlessly about soybeans and all of their intricacies. But that morning at the family soy sauce factory, I was in no mood to chat. The only thing on my mind was the ninety-degree heat. Heat rose from the ground through my thin-soled flats; it filled my nostrils, mouth, and ears. Sweat bloomed under my arms, in the creases of my elbows, in the pockets behind my knees. Even in the shade, beneath the factory's red-striped awning, the air felt thick enough to drink. Flanked by my father and my uncle, I shifted my weight from one swollen foot to another and wished the clients would hurry up and get here.

In the last three months, I'd turned thirty, gotten separated from my husband, and prepared to take a hiatus from San Francisco, my home of fifteen years. Now it was August. I'd been back in Singapore and living in my parents' house for the past week. At my father's urging, I'd agreed to temp at the factory, taking on mundane administrative tasks that had little to do with soy sauce. Even though I'd held this new job for exactly four days, my inexperience hadn't stopped my father from insisting I attend this meeting.

Forming a visor with the flat of my hand, I squinted at the logo embedded in the center of the compound gate: thick brushstrokes that formed, 林, the Chinese character for my family name. Since the founding of Lin's Soy Sauce by my grandfather fifty years earlier, the factory had grown into a gated campus with three squat concrete buildings surrounding a central courtyard. The architecture was spare and utilitarian, almost ascetic, as though any kind of ornamentation would distract from the task of creating soy sauce. My father, my uncle, and I were standing on the steps of the building that housed the office staff, and each time the glass door swung open, a wave of air conditioning rushed out, providing temporary relief from the heat.

If my father noticed my discomfort, he chose to ignore it. He checked his old-fashioned flip phone for missed calls. He removed his glasses and began to polish them on the edge of his shirt. Stripped of their familiar shield, Ba's eyes looked puffy and helpless. When he caught me watching, he smiled. Tiny lines radiated outward from his temples as if etched into his skin with a fine-toothed comb. It was a simple smile, involuntary—the kind of smile you flashed at a toddler wearing a funny hat—and in spite of myself, I smiled back.

On my other side, my uncle pulled an already limp handkerchief from his pocket and swiped it across the back of his neck. Where Ba was wiry and compact, Uncle Robert was tall and wide by Singaporean standards, with an ample belly perched precariously atop his belt. He grinned at me. "Hot, right?" he asked cheerfully. He reached over and squeezed my father's bicep. "Gretchen is A-mah-ri-can now," he said, elongating the word and chuckling. "Can no longer *tahan* the heat."

Singaporeans take perverse pride in the local climate, where temperatures rise to the high eighties year round and never dip below seventy-five degrees. Our tiny island sits off the southernmost tip of the Malaysian Peninsula in Southeast Asia, just one degree shy of the equator. In polite conversation, we'll tell you we have two seasons: hot-and-wet and hot-and-dry. In less polite conversation, we'll reveal there are three: hot, very hot, and very fucking hot. During my time in the Bay Area, I learned to keep my mouth shut when my American friends complained of the humidity. Standing there on the front steps with my silk blouse pasted to my back, I thought of crisp San Francisco fall days, of warm sunlight on cold skin.

I was about to launch into a new round of protests when a long, dark car glided through the gate and pulled into a spot. Two men stepped out. The older was short with slicked-back white hair atop a head that seemed too large for his slight body. The younger was slim but broad shouldered and taller than his companion, though the height discrepancy could have been due in part to his hair, which he wore gelled up in a subtle fauxhawk. I'd noticed this hairstyle on other young Singaporean men, and before that on fashion-forward members of the San Francisco gay community, and I found it too contrived to be stylish. Aside from his hair, the younger man's most distinguishing feature was a pair of glossy black spectacles, slim around the lenses and broad at the temples, which so complemented his face they seemed to be part of him, as inextricable as a nose or an ear.

Since returning home, I'd renounced all but the most basic forms of grooming. Now, I tried not to think about my scraggly shoulder-length strands, or the bags under my eyes, or the way my lips remained cracked beneath layers of ChapStick.

Ba and Uncle Robert had already briefed me on the visitors. Kendro Santoso ran a chain of upscale Pan-Asian restaurants all over Southeast Asia — Jakarta, where he was based, Bangkok, Kuala Lumpur, Manila, and, now, Singapore. The latest Spice Alley was slated to open at the Shangri-La Hotel within the year. Mr. Santoso was taking a tour of the plant before he decided whether to sign an exclusive wholesale contract with Lin's Soy Sauce. My father and uncle thought it would be interesting for me to participate, and naturally, I disagreed.

As a child, I'd loved coming to the factory with my father on Saturday mornings. I'd spent many a family dinner listening to the grown-ups debate the virtues of cedar- versus oak-barrel aging. At thirteen, I'd even spent the June school holidays working on the bottling line, as my cousin Cal had before me. But that grueling job only strengthened my resolve never to enter the family trade. That was the last time I'd worked at Lin's. I'd learned nothing since. I knew little about what my father and uncle actually did. But Ba dismissed my concerns. He assured me that none of my assignments were urgent; the other admins would manage just fine without me.

Mr. Santoso came toward Uncle Robert with his hand extended. He apologized for being late even though he was right on time; then, he introduced his son, his youngest. He was called James.

"And this is Gretchen, my daughter," said my father. "Just home from America."

I clamped my arms to my sides in an attempt to hide the sweat stains.

"She's very bright," Uncle Robert added, as if describing a puppy or a small child. He leaned in close like he was sharing a secret. "Graduated from Stanford." He didn't mention that I was on leave from the San Francisco Conservatory, and I wasn't surprised.

"James went to New York University for his MBA," Mr. Santoso said. "On the other coast." He gave a shouting laugh like this was the punch line of a joke. If he was wondering about Cal, Uncle Robert's absent son, he was too polite to ask.

Relieved, my uncle and father laughed, too. The son grinned indulgently at his father. He had an easy air about him, endemic to the kind of guy who glided through life — the kind of guy who had a well-bred, fine-boned, Chinese girlfriend waiting for him to propose, which made me wonder if I looked as tired and haggard as I felt, like the kind of girl whose American husband had left her for his twenty-one-year-old undergraduate research assistant, a detail I had withheld from classmates, friends, and especially family.

"Let's begin," Uncle Robert said, holding the door open and beckoning us into the air-conditioned lobby.

As we moved down a corridor lined with framed black-and-white photographs, I paused at my favorite, which showed my grandfather with a full head of silver hair and the lopsided grin that had been passed through my father to me. In the picture, Ahkong was bending over to scoop a handful of fermented bean mush from a large clay jar. Once he'd given me a taste straight from his hand, and my mouth still watered when I remembered the sharp acidity of that single bite.

Up ahead, my uncle was explaining the history of Lin's Soy Sauce to our guests, a story that was recounted in my family at least once a year, more so now that my cousins' children were old enough to understand. Although I knew all the details by heart, I always paid attention, watching the children's faces, wishing they could have heard it first hand from Ahkong.

My grandfather — Lin Ming Tek to his employees, Ahkong to us grandkids — began his career at Yellow River, the Hong Kong soy sauce giant responsible for the mass-produced stuff that all us Lins learned at a young age to abhor. After Ahkong rose quickly through the ranks and became head of the Singapore division, the president of Yellow River flew him to Hong Kong and treated him to a celebratory dinner at the best restaurant in town — a restaurant finer than anything on the sleepy island of Singapore. Here, at this fine restaurant, Ahkong had his first taste of real soy sauce, poured by a waistcoat-clad waiter into a porcelain dish small enough to sit in the palm of his hand. Shimmering and lively with a smooth, dry finish, this sauce was a sparkling stream to Yellow River's murky, stagnant, pond-water brew.

Despite his recent promotion, and with it, the guarantee of a comfortable life, Ahkong made up his mind to open his own factory, one that would produce naturally fermented soy sauce, made from the highest-quality ingredients.

Accomplishing this goal meant mastering an entirely new production method — one that was quickly becoming obsolete. The companies that produced the majority of soy sauces had all taken the same short cuts, using chemicals to speed up fermentation and increasing salt content to mask inferior ingredients. Only a few factories continued to practice the ancient technique of naturally aging soybeans in century-old barrels. This process yielded the delicate, multifaceted golden broth that had long enhanced the flavors of Asian cuisine, and now Ahkong was determined to bring this treasure to Singapore. As part of his education, he apprenticed with the Chiba Soy Sauce Factory, a premier artisanal soy sauce maker located on the island of Shodoshima, in Japan's Seto Inland Sea. There he learned traditional Japanese techniques that he would apply to his own special brand of Chinese soy sauce.

My uncle's condensed version skipped ahead several years to my grandfather's long list of successes and accolades. He made it sound simple, like getting discovered by a Hollywood director in a supermarket parking lot. But I knew the truth.

Before she'd passed away, my grandmother had confided her side of the story. Amah's version stressed her dismay at discovering that her husband had quit his lucrative job and was planning to leave

Singapore and his family for six months to pursue some obscure, romantic dream.

"This was the fifties, mind you," Amah would say in Chinese, knowing those numbers meant nothing to us grandkids. Undeterred, she continued. "The country was in chaos, what with the race riots, and the Communists and the Nationalists and the pro-British Chinese — no, we weren't even a country yet." Here, she caught herself and shook her head. "Singapore wasn't the way it was today. I know you little melons will find this hard to believe, but the whole island was a mess. Absolutely filthy — squatters everywhere, chickens and pigs running loose."

She was right; I couldn't imagine my spotless, perfectly manicured city overrun by rambunctious farm animals. Cal, perhaps ten or eleven, glanced up from his comic book and then resumed reading. His younger siblings Lily and Rose pretended to listen while they carried on their own private conversation by exchanging looks. Only I, too accustomed to playing on my own to join the girls, too juvenile to be of interest to Cal, was truly intrigued.

According to Amah, Ahkong had worked every day of his life to give his family a good, stable home, and now he was throwing it all away — and to go to Japan, of all places. "Less than a decade after the war. What would people think!"

She pleaded with him to stay — she even threatened to leave him — but my grandfather was stubborn. He demanded, then debated, then begged Amah to let him go. While she considered her decision, he neither ate nor slept, but sat forlornly at his desk, teaching himself Japanese.

"What could I do?" Amah asked, her outrage tempered by time. "He had already quit his job. His moping was driving us crazy. I told him if he didn't return in exactly six months, he would never hold his sons again."

Upon seeing my wide eyes and dropped jaw, Amah stroked my hair and reassured me that this had been an empty threat. "Of course, I could never have done that to our boys."

My grandmother wasn't the only one who questioned Ahkong's sanity. His former colleagues told him there was no money to be made in this fancy sauce. Customers wouldn't be able to tell the difference, and they certainly wouldn't fork over the extra cash.

But the more my grandfather learned, the more determined he grew.

Now, Uncle Robert paused to make sure he still had our guests' full attention. "Once people saw how a single teaspoon can bring out the fragrance of scallion and ginger and garlic, or how a light coating can amplify the smokiness of tender roast meat," —here, he bunched up his fingertips and brought them to his lips— "how could they turn away?"

Our guests nodded solemnly. My father's eyes twinkled at me from behind his glasses, and I wished he would stop trying to engage me. I appreciated the effort, really, I did, but I was dealing with the time difference, the weather, the pain that slashed through me when I thought of all I'd left behind. Slapping a grin across my face, nodding my head to demonstrate interest—these acts required energy I did not have.

Besides, Ba needed to relax. He was technically retired: my mother's worsening health had pushed him to let his younger brother take over as Lin's president. This past week, however, with Cal still away, my father had come in to work every day after shuttling Ma to and from dialysis treatments. She'd been a professor of German literature at the National University of Singapore before kidney failure had forced her to resign. She was not interested in soy sauce.

Uncle Robert was telling the Santosos that it was only a matter of time before soy sauce overtook ketchup and mustard to become the number one condiment in America.

"It's definitely possible," Mr. Santoso said. "The Americans do love Asian food. When I was a student in Michigan, you couldn't order fish that wasn't deep fried. Now there's sushi in every supermarket. Isn't that right, Son? Isn't that something?"

"It's something all right," the son said. He spoke with an American accent — typical rich kid who'd grown up in private, international schools.

To be fair, I was often mistaken for a native Californian, but I also spoke fluent Singlish, and thought of my accents like different hats, or maybe wigs, to be donned depending on occasion and mood. Still, even as I dismissed the son, his slurred syllables and flattened vowels and dropped consonants sent a tiny thrill through my body, like that moment you catch sight of a friend you haven't seen in years and can't decide whether to call out or slink away.

We followed Uncle Robert out to the cement-paved courtyard, which held rows and rows of Lin's proprietary clay jars, each one large enough for a child to crouch inside. When we reached a patch of shade beneath a spindly yellow flame tree, my uncle explained that all seventy waist-high vessels had been custom-made for Ahkong in China's Fujian province. The jars contained a mixture of whole soybeans — steamed instead of boiled to retain their earthy flavor — sea salt, water, and roasted winter wheat. Every four days, a worker stirred the contents of each jar with a long wooden paddle.

Aside from this intervention, the covered jars were left to naturally ferment, beneath the sun, for five to six months.

On the opposite end of the courtyard, in the shadow of the shed that hid Lin's new fiberglass tanks from view, a skinny, slightly stooped, older man was monitoring jar temperatures with a dial thermometer. He was dressed like the factory workers in a bright yellow polo shirt with our logo—a ring-enclosed 林—plastered across the back. Even before I saw his face, I recognized Mr. Liu, Lin's head scientist. He nodded at me furtively, not wanting to attract attention, and I raised my hand and waggled my fingers.

But Uncle Robert jumped at the opportunity to introduce our guests to Lin's oldest employee, hired by Ahkong back in 1958. "Lucky he's been with us ever since. We couldn't survive without him." He waved Mr. Liu over and clapped him on the back. "*Ng dao eh sai bo?*"

Shielding his eyes from the sun, Mr. Liu answered in Chinese that the fermentation process was going just fine. He pointed an index finger skyward, stretched his lips into a shy smile and switched to English for the benefit of the visitors. "Hot days, *hor*, bad for people, good for beans."

Beside me, James looked remarkably unruffled by the heat. His poreless skin was moisture free, his shirt collar crisp as card stock. He squinted at the sky and inhaled deeply. "Smells like a brewery," he said to no one in particular. When he raised one corner of his mouth, I looked away.

As we made our way back to the offices, James fell in step beside me. "So," he said, "what kind of work do you do around here?"

"Oh," I said, feeling the heat settle on my cheeks, "Nothing important. I'm really just here to pass time." I considered explaining that I was taking the semester off from graduate school to help care for my mother. Instead, I quickened my pace to catch up to the others, who were discussing a company that a mutual friend had been forced to sell.

"It's always best when a business can stay in the family, though certainly there are challenges," Mr. Santoso said. He gestured to his son. "So far, I've been quite fortunate."

Uncle Robert and Ba made vague sounds of agreement. Neither, I could tell, wanted to discuss these challenges in greater detail.

In a low voice James said, "I apologize for my dad. He can be a little prosaic at times."

I tried to remember what "prosaic" meant as I searched for a funny response. When our fathers moved out of hearing distance, I said, "Mine's the king of misused idioms. He's coined such gems as 'talking about the devil,' and, oh—in college, he used to call me a 'party dog.'" Even though this was true, I felt guilty for making fun of Ba while he was standing right there.

When James laughed, his entire face shifted, creasing his forehead, wrinkling his nose and the corners of his eyes. A small pleasurable ache spread through my lower abdomen, a tightening that just as quickly slackened, leaving me invigorated and bemused. Suddenly I questioned why I so indiscriminately craved the approval of others.

An electronic rendering of the Queen of the Night's aria pierced the air: my new cell phone ring. Everyone turned. My father frowned.

"I'm sorry," I said, rooting around in the handbag I'd purchased precisely for its multiple pockets and compartments. "Nobody here's a Mozart fan?"

Only James gave an uncomfortable chuckle. I silenced the queen by thumbing the red button, but not before I caught the name that flashed across the screen: Paul.

I did the math. Ten a.m. here made it five p.m. in San Francisco. We hadn't spoken since I'd left a week earlier, and our last conversation had been terse. I couldn't think of any reason for him to be calling me now. But then, perhaps he had no reason; perhaps he just wanted to hear my voice.

"Xiao Xi," my father called from the top of the stairs, using my Chinese nickname. There was an edge to his tone.

The others were already in the conference room, so I hurried to join them.

Inside the room, one of the administrative assistants was pouring whole-leaf Iron Goddess of Mercy tea into five cerulean-blue teacups. My uncle sat at the head of the long table beneath a pair of Chinese landscape scrolls, featuring vast, jagged mountains overlooking a fog-shrouded river. He gestured for me to take the chair beside my father and across from James. "Now we will try some sauce," he said.

At the center of the table stood two slender glass bottles bearing gold labels embossed with the ring-enclosed 林. A squat plastic bottle of Yellow River, the sauce produced by Ahkong's former employer, had been set to one side, separated from its more graceful counterparts by a white porcelain tray containing three separate sauce compartments. Next to it was a dish of rice crackers the size and shape of communion wafers.

My father had led me through my first tasting at the age of six, and every year following, until I reached the age when kids start to hate everything their parents want them to like. Now, eighteen years later, the same impatience I'd felt as a girl of twelve washed over me. I wanted nothing more than to jump out of my seat, return to my desk, and call Paul.

But Ba was going to give our guests the full experience, and because I knew what was at stake for Lin's, I paid attention.

He flipped up the cap of the Yellow River bottle and poured the sauce into the first compartment. "We start with the lousy stuff," he said with a wink, and then his face grew serious. He held up the tray and swirled the sauce around with a priest's solemnity. "You can see how dark that is?" he asked, his eyes narrowing in distaste.

The Santosos studied the tray as if it were a Rorschach test. I, however, knew what to look for. The sauce was dense and opaque and left a brown-black stain on the porcelain like a watery thumbprint.

Ba placed the tray back on the table and instructed the Santosos to lean in. "A bit closer, *lah*. Get a good sniff." He took three short deep inhales to demonstrate. Just like a dog, he used to say when I was younger.

James bowed his head, exposing his fauxhawk in a manner that struck me as almost vulgar, a too-gummy smile in an otherwise pretty face. I wondered how much gel he slicked on each morning to make his hair stand up that way. I could feel the oily stickiness beneath my palms.

"You too, Xiao Xi," Ba said, pushing the tray toward me.

I bowed my head, and the sharp, acrid smell of Yellow River made me grimace.

Next, Ba picked up a cracker, dunked its tip in the sauce and indicated that the rest of us should follow. The sauce tasted exactly like it smelled.

"Harsh, flat, one-dimensional. Almost metallic aftertaste," my uncle said, shaking his head. "Terrible, *lah,* this sauce. It doesn't matter how good your ingredients are if you cook with this."

Ba added, "This isn't real soy sauce. The color and flavor come from chemical."

My mother's voice flashed in my head, her American accent honed over years spent studying in Ithaca, New York. "Chemicals, Xiong," she corrected. "Chemicals with an *s.*" Ba often confused the singular and plural, which didn't exist in Chinese.

Next we moved on to the two bottles of Lin's soy sauce. My uncle taught the Santosos to take a small sip of each sauce, rolling the liquid over their tongues to experience all the flavors. After the previous mouthful, this sauce was a revelation. Times like this, I understood why my grandfather had risked so much in pursuit of the perfect brew.

"Real soy sauce is as complex as a fine wine — fruity, earthy, floral also can, *lah.*" Uncle Robert pointed out the lively acidity of the light soy sauce in comparison to the rich, mellow sweetness of the dark one. Light soy, he explained, was used for seasoning and dipping; dark soy was used for cooking because its flavors developed under heat.

James and his father crimped their brows and made sucking noises with their tongues against their teeth. If Paul were here, he would have nudged me under the table. He hated any kind of pretension. A bunch of shee-shaws, he called people he considered phony. When I asked how he'd come up with that, he sat up very straight and lengthened his face like a bloodhound and muttered, "Shee-shaw shee-shaw shee-shaw," as he wagged his head in time.

But Ba and Uncle Robert observed the Santosos' display with approval. So many years and so many tastings later, no one could accuse them of not caring about their work.

When the Santosos' questions were answered, and my father was satisfied that they appreciated the discrepancies between Yellow River's and our sauces, he left the conference room and returned with a tray of tall glasses and three cold, sweating cans of Sprite. "Now for a special treat," he said.

The Santosos looked so eager that my allegiances flipped, and I silently chastised Paul. Why was he so threatened by other people? My irritation must have registered on my face because my father threw me a questioning glance. I only shook my head.

Ba poured out the Sprite and tipped in a dash of dark soy sauce. The caramel streak swirled through the glass like an ominous cloud.

James and his father traded uneasy looks. They held their glasses to the light.

"Try it, *lah*," Ba said.

"You'll like it," said Uncle Robert.

"No, really, it's delicious," I said.

The three of us watched as the Santosos raised their glasses to their lips and sipped gingerly, their eyes widening in delight.

My father pushed the third glass to me, and I took a long drink. The mixture, Ahkong's creation, was sweet and tangy and savory—a comforting, full-bodied flavor like burnt sugar, or brown butter that contrasted sharply with the dancing bubbles on my tongue.

When Mr. Santoso reached the bottom of his glass, my uncle

moved right in with the pricing sheet, pointing out the special discount Lin's was offering for the first time ever. At the mention of
the discount, I thought I saw my father flinch, but the next time I
checked, his brow was smooth. He was a professional.

James pulled out a mobile device and began to tap at the screen.
After a moment, he tipped the screen to his father.

"This is all very impressive," said Mr. Santoso.

Ba and Uncle Robert inched forward in their chairs.

"But, with all that's happened this month," Mr. Santoso continued, "we do have some small concerns."

Before he could say more, my uncle said, "Let me assure you, I
will personally handle your account. There will be no oversights.
You have my word."

Again, Mr. Santoso studied his son's mini screen.

James's gaze lifted toward me, and I realized I was holding my
breath. Avoiding his eyes, I focused on the paintings on the wall behind Uncle Robert's head. There, in the very bottom corner of one
scroll, amid the towering mountains and winding river, partially
hidden by a large boulder, was a tiny thumbnail-size man in a tiny
fishing boat.

At last Mr. Santoso put down the device. He extended his hand to
my uncle and smiled with his entire face. "I look forward to serving
your soy sauce in our restaurants."

The walls of the conference room seemed to expand with our
collective exhale. We rose to our feet, and after a round of handshakes, my uncle called for an assistant to bring out a case of Lin's
prize-winning oyster sauce for our guests to take with them. Then
we escorted them to their car, where we entered into another round
of handshakes.

"How much longer are you in town?" my father asked, pumping Mr. Santoso's arm with gusto.

"Just until the weekend, though we're back and forth a lot from Jakarta. We have a condo in River Valley where James spends most of his time."

"Any time you want to discuss business, give us a call," said my uncle. "No question is too small."

"That's very kind," James said, gazing over my uncle's shoulder at me.

I dropped my head and felt my heartbeat in my temples. I blamed Ba and Uncle Robert—for using me to distract these men from Cal's absence, for trying so hard to make me care.

Finally the Santosos drove off, and Ba and Uncle Robert congratulated each other, taking turns to thump me on the back. Only then did I fully appreciate how tense they'd been.

"You know-*ah*, Gretch," Uncle Robert said, "when you were small, you used to love coming to the factory. You knew all the workers' names." He'd told this story before—how I'd spent so much time on the factory floor that Mr. Liu had given me my own yellow polo shirt, so I could look like everyone else.

Right on cue, my father said, "That shirt came down to your knee. You wore it every week for an entire year."

They often conversed like this, as if engaged in some sort of call-and-response.

Now, it was Uncle Robert's turn. "Remember how she loved those rice snacks?" He was referring to the crackers used for tastings.

"At home you ate nothing," Ba said, "but here you would eat an entire packet if I didn't stop you." He looped an arm around me as we walked back inside, and without thinking, I slid out from beneath him.

It had been a long time since I'd viewed the factory as my own personal playground, but I didn't bother to point this out. My head was filled with other thoughts. His name lit up in my mind as it had on my cell phone: Paul-paul-paul — an endless chain of hope and history, falling off the screen, slipping out of reach.

2

BACK IN 1958, when my grandfather opened his new soy
sauce factory, he mandated that all employees, factory and
office staff alike, break each day at 12:30 for a family-style
meal prepared by in-house cooks. By the time I began temping at
Lin's, Ahkong had been gone for five years, but along with his custom-made jars and secret recipes, the practice of staff lunches had
lived on to the extent that his favorite southern Chinese dishes were
still in rotation: braised pork with hard-boiled eggs, stewed chicken
with black mushrooms, sweet potato porridge. Many of these dishes
I'd missed dearly during my time in San Francisco, and yet lunch
was an activity I tried my best to avoid.

My first day at work, I slipped into the kitchen early to fill a plate
to take upstairs, but my uncle spotted me on my way out and insisted
I take the seat beside him to explain what exactly I was learning
in this master's program in music education. After that, I feigned
stomach trouble and stayed at my desk, where I ate Cinnamon

Toast Crunch — purchased at the expat grocery store for twice the price — straight from the box.

Now, as I headed back to my desk from the parking lot, people streamed past me toward the dining room. I spotted Fiona and Shuting, administrative assistants who I'd worked with over the past week, and, for the sake of conversation, asked where they were going.

"To *makan*," Shuting said. She mimed spooning food from the cupped bowl of her palm.

Even though I certainly would have declined, I waited for them to invite me, and when neither did, I tried to look busy by hustling back to my office.

My inability to make friends at work, I believed, could be traced back to this spacious room with freshly painted, pale-pistachio walls, right next door to my father's corner office. As if things weren't awkward enough with my last name plastered across every bottle we shipped out, I'd also earned the distinction of being the only temp in the history of the company to land her own office. I'd pleaded with my uncle for a regular cubicle, but he'd waved a hand at the window that overlooked the dense configuration of workspaces on the office floor. "Where do you want me to put you? This place is already packed, and that friend of yours arrives next week."

He was referring to Frankie Shepherd, my old college roommate, who was about to start a yearlong consultant position at Lin's — a job I'd helped her obtain back when neither of us expected that I, too, would be in Singapore, much less just across the hall. At least Frankie would also have an office. Still, in protest, I refused to hang pictures on my wall, or to bring in photographs or potted plants. Whenever my uncle or father commented on the sparseness of the decor, I took the opportunity to remind them that I was only temping for a few months. Come January, I'd be back at the conservatory, completing my last semester.

A knock interrupted my thoughts, and Shuting pushed open the door without waiting for a response. She was a skinny girl with a shrill voice and a mouth that was perpetually in motion.

"By the way," she said as though we were in the middle of a conversation, "you got a phone call while you were gone. Someone named Paul."

She was waiting for a reaction, and I willed myself to stay calm. Paul had a name for girls like her, too: drama vultures. This office was filled with them.

"Oh?" I said with a shrug. "Did he leave a message?"

Disappointed, Shuting sighed. "He just said to call him back. Sorry-*ah*, forgot to tell you."

I gave her a brisk nod. "Anything else?"

She shook her head.

When the door closed behind her, I picked up the phone, weighing its heft in my palm. Paul must have called the house first and spoken to my mother. Who else would have told him how to reach me here? A line of tension moved through me, like someone zipping me up from my tailbone to the tip of my spine. Paul and my mother had always gotten along. Surely she would have pressed him for information, and while I knew he'd honor our agreement to keep the details of our separation to ourselves, the thought of them conversing—asking after each other, showing concern—made my hands shake.

I dropped the handset in its cradle and reached for the cereal box in my bottom drawer—the same cereal I ate for breakfast, right here at my desk, to avoid sitting down at the dining table with my parents. I shoveled a handful in my mouth and chewed, shoveled and chewed, savoring the heady burst of sweetness, the hearty preservative-enhanced crunch, the American excess of it all. Turning to my computer, I clicked on a new email from Kat Tan, my oldest friend in Singapore. It was an invitation to her thirtieth birthday party, and I closed the message to avoid having to make a decision.

In the hallway outside my office, a girl from the marketing department paused at my window and made a show of shuffling through a stack of documents while keeping one eye on my strange mealtime ritual. I went over and yanked the cord to lower the blinds.

Minutes later, a sharp rap on my door. I yanked it open with too much force and came face to face with my father. "Oh," I said. "It's you."

"Everything all right?" he asked. His gaze scanned the room before landing on the cereal box.

"Everything's fine," I said, returning to my chair. "Except the entire company seems to think I'm some kind of exotic animal. This office might as well be a cage at the zoo."

Ba's smile fell short of his eyes. "They'll get bored soon enough." He glanced over again at the cereal, but wisely avoided mentioning it. "I'm going home to pick up Ma." He adjusted his glasses on his nose. "For her doctor's appointment." He waited, daring me to speak.

I shifted my gaze to my computer screen and placed one hand on the mouse. "Okay."

He stood there with his arms crossed, and then whirled around and opened the door. Before I could relax he stuck his head back in.

"Coming home for dinner or not?" he asked, as if I hadn't given the same answer three days in a row.

"Not tonight."

As soon as my father's steps had receded down the hall, I heard whispers and giggles right outside my door. I pictured the marketing girl on the other side, by now no doubt joined by several others, their eyes widening with curiosity — even glee. I longed to fling the phone across the room so it would strike the door with a deafening crack. And then I longed for the anonymity of my life in San Francisco, where I was nobody's daughter, granddaughter, cousin, niece.

I folded my arms on my desk, lay my head down and wished I were anywhere else but this bare office, surrounded by hushed voices and watchful eyes. I couldn't imagine how much worse the gossip would be if they'd known about Paul's affair; I couldn't imagine my father's slow-burning rage had he known, too.

When I finally made myself leave my office, I found Shuting huddled with Fiona in her cube, replaying the online video of my cousin Cal's interview with a local news anchor. I too had seen the clip my first day home. Already privy to how the scandal had unfolded, I'd watched horrified as my cousin looked the news anchor straight in the eye and told her slowly and clearly that he was only going to repeat himself one more time: he, and Lin's, had done nothing wrong. Shortly after that interview, my father had ordered Cal to leave town.

Upon noticing me, Fiona quickly closed the webpage.

Shuting was the first to recover. With exaggerated concern she asked, "Why you always skip lunch? You managed to call Paul or not?"

I didn't even want her to say his name. When I didn't respond, Fiona studied my face and asked if I was feeling okay. She was a serious, sensibly dressed woman whom I thought of as middle-aged even though she was probably only a few years older than I am. I was relieved when Jason from sales peeked his head around the side of the cube, saving me from having to answer.

"Apparently *xiao lao ban* is back in town," he said, taking up everyone's favorite topic of discussion: Cal, who was known as "little boss" behind his back. Jason's face fell when he saw me. "Oh," he said, "you're here."

In the years I'd been abroad, discarding jobs and collecting graduate degrees, my cousin had stayed firmly in one spot, determined to learn everything he could about the family business. Ever since Cal was a teenager he'd spent his school holidays working at the factory. All through university he'd interned in the sales department. Even during his two and a half years of mandatory military service, he'd regularly drop by the office in full uniform. Upon graduation, when Cal was made Lin's vice president, no one was surprised.

Months earlier, my cousin had begun his latest push to bring the company into the new millennium with a line of ready-to-cook sauces in such flavors as teriyaki, sweet and sour, black bean, and Peking duck. Although Uncle Robert and Ba had reservations, Cal pointed out that Lin's was already experimenting with cheaper, fiberglass-aged soy sauce. He argued that this new line of condiments would only bolster the company's efforts to reach a younger demographic. Sure enough, early consumer feedback was overwhelmingly positive and orders rolled in faster than they could be filled.

One week after the launch, the first report of food poisoning came in from Rice Broker, a small fast-food chain, not at all like the upscale restaurants that purchased Lin's soy sauce.

Cal must have panicked when he saw he had a potentially serious problem on his hands, especially since it had been his decision to streamline the production process by cutting out several hygiene measures. But only three or four more complaints trickled in, and the source of contamination remained difficult to isolate. In the meantime, sales of the new sauces continued to outpace forecasts by two to one. Recalling the line of sauces at this point would not only come at huge cost, but would harm the company's reputation — perhaps unnecessarily. Cal must have told himself all this when he opted to keep the food-poisoning reports a secret. Drawing on the largest marketing budget in the history of the company, he continued to aggressively promote his new products.

At first, it appeared he'd gambled correctly. No other cases of food poisoning emerged. But then a *Straits Times* reporter fell ill after eating a plate of sliced cod stir-fried in Lin's black bean ready-to-cook sauce. The reporter interviewed a friend who had served the sauce to her family, and whose toddler had projectile vomited for twelve hours. The reporter began to investigate, going so far as to send a sample of the black bean sauce to the Ministry of Health. His article exposed Lin's shortcuts on the production line and questioned not only Cal's management abilities but also his sense of decency. How could a company that claimed to uphold family values continue to sell a product that made people sick? The reporter ended with the Chinese proverb: Wealth does not pass three generations. By the time the article landed on newsstands, it didn't matter that the ministry's tests had been inconclusive.

My mother was the one who called me in San Francisco and kept me abreast of the latest developments; my father was too furious and exhausted to talk about it.

Eventually, Ba and Uncle Robert recalled all remaining products at enormous cost to the company. They killed the new line and placed Cal on a leave of absence while they worked to salvage the company's reputation. Now, two weeks into my cousin's exile, Ba and Uncle Robert were still in the process of determining Cal's future at Lin's — a discussion they kept closely guarded.

Their silence only encouraged more speculation among the office staff.

"If he's back in town, he'll be here next week," said Shuting.

"Unless he *kena* sacked over the weekend," said Jason, wiggling his eyebrows lewdly. His eyes darted toward me, and he ducked his head. "Sorry-*ah*."

I waved away his apology. Cal deserved to be disparaged.

"They won't sack him," Fiona said firmly.

All three of them politely refrained from making the obvious cracks about the beauty of nepotism. They waited for me to speak.

Weakly I said, "I heard he spent his entire leave diving in the Maldives," and they looked unimpressed.

Jason asked if my father had revealed anything else about Cal to me, and when I assured them I had no additional information, Shuting dismissed me with a shake of her head. "Yah, *lah*, whatever," she said. "Confidentiality rules and all that, right?" In Chinese, she said to the others, "Of course she can't tell us," knowing full well I understood.

We heard my uncle's door swing open, and Jason and Shuting got up to leave, but not before the three of them agreed to go for beers at the hawker center after work. I wasn't invited to come along.

Fiona handed me a box of envelopes to stuff for a mass mailing and said in a low voice, "Don't let those two bother you. They anyhow *qit gong bueh gong*, but they don't know anything."

I smiled to show her I was fine.

In my office, I printed fifty copies of a form letter to our best clients, thanking them for their continued loyalty through this difficult time, and sat down to work. Usually I enjoyed these mindless repetitive tasks: entering data into Excel spreadsheets, organizing files, making photocopies. But this afternoon I couldn't focus. I folded and unfolded each letter, convinced I'd misaddressed its envelope.

Outside my window, beyond the low rooftops of the factory, the downtown skyscrapers gleamed like pyrite beneath the midafternoon sun. Polished, spotless, sterile.

In San Francisco, I'd fallen in love with the crumbling Victorian neighborhoods, some of which had lived through multiple earthquakes. Paul's and my Russian Hill apartment building dated back to 1922.

"Just means we'll be safe when the next earthquake comes," Paul said as our building's cramped cage elevator lifted us into the air. That night, three years into our marriage, we discovered that yanking back the door stopped the elevator in its tracks. As the elevator hung suspended between the third and fourth floors, I peeled off my sweater and let it fall to the grimy floor before pulling him to me, pressing my mouth to his neck. I'd unbuttoned his shirt and was reaching for his belt buckle when an unmistakable voice boomed down from above. "You two better not be doing what I think you're doing." It was our next-door neighbor, Mrs. O'Donley.

Giggling uncontrollably, we pulled on our clothes, smoothed our hair, and tried to compose ourselves by the time the elevator opened on the fifth floor. The old lady stood there with her hands on her hips.

"Good evening, Mrs. O'Donley," Paul said, bending at the waist to look her in the eye. "I'm so sorry about the wait." He bared two rows of teeth, shiny and white as domino tiles.

"Oh," she said, taking a step back. Her cheeks colored, her jaw softened. No doubt all would have been forgiven if I hadn't burst into another round of giggles.

Mrs. O'Donley recovered. "Some of us have places to be," she said, peering sternly over her glasses.

We hurried into our apartment, and he collapsed on the bed, dragging me down on top of him, and together we laughed until we were clutching our stomachs.

Later that night, when we made love, I pulled Paul against me as hard as I could, again and again, bruising my hipbones, crushing my ribs. He thought I was just really turned on, but that wasn't it: I'd awakened a longing I could not control, an awareness of the spaces he could not fill.

The clock on my computer said three in the afternoon. One a.m. in California. I pictured Paul pacing the length of his new apartment with his cell phone pressed to his ear, asking about my mother's health, telling her about his research. I heard him suck in his breath when she lowered her voice to signal a change of subject, and said, "Be straight with me, Paul. Is it really over between you two?" Did he throw out something vague and meaningless like, "These things are complicated"? Did he chew on the insides of his cheeks before confessing that he truly didn't know?

I was stuffing my last few envelopes when the phone rang. I held my breath, but it was only Ba. Then I remembered he was calling from the doctor's.

It was supposed to have been a routine checkup, and he tried to assure me that everything was fine, even though the doctor had run tests and Ma's potassium level was higher than normal. When further questioned, Ba conceded that this condition could be dangerous if left untreated, so the doctor was keeping her at the hospital overnight just to be safe.

"You know how Dr. Yeoh is," he said. "Very cautious one, *lah*."

"But what happened?" I repeated, annoyed by his efforts to placate me, determined to have my suspicions confirmed. "What caused this?"

He finally admitted that Ma might have had a gin and tonic or two while lunching with a friend that afternoon — he was hazy on the details, and I bit my lip to hold back the wave of accusations.

I dropped the stuffed envelopes off at Fiona's desk and explained I had to leave early. As I walked down the hall to the stairwell, I heard Shuting scurry over to Fiona's cube. I didn't turn back to catch her in the act.

It was no secret that my mother's chronic kidney disease had deteriorated into full-fledged kidney failure, but what my co-workers didn't know — what I was only just beginning to grasp — was the extent to which Ma's drinking was compromising her health. Forced to retire at age fifty-eight, Ma now spent the majority of her days chained to a dialysis machine, a routine that would probably continue for the rest of her life. In some ways I couldn't fault her for needing to fill those lonely, empty hours. Since I was a child, Ma had always enjoyed an after-work cocktail, a glass or two of good wine, and yet thanks to my father's deft orchestrations, she never appeared anything more than charmingly tipsy. In recent years, however, there were more incidents he couldn't explain away, like the time she phoned me long-distance in the middle of the night, her voice too loud and strangely shrill. "Do love me, ducky?" she'd slurred into the phone. "Do you really, truly love me?"

In the car on my way to the Gleneagles Hospital, my guilt bubbled out of me. My father never asked for help, it wasn't his way, but Ma needed something he could not provide. I resolved to show I was here for them, ready to play a more active role in her care.

Three months earlier, I'd called to tell my parents' the most bareboned version of my separation from Paul: our marriage wasn't working, he was moving out. I braced myself for the barrage of questions, but all I heard was silence; I thought my cell phone might have dropped the call. Then Ba said, "We have news, too. Ma's going on dialysis." He waited three days before suggesting, carefully, that perhaps it was time to come home, and at that moment, thinking only of myself, I felt relief.

Consumed by Ma's health problems and Cal's betrayal, my father had yet to push me to explain my separation, but I lived in a constant state of dread.

I emerged from the elevator on the hospital's ninth floor. Despite my best intentions, when I saw my father pacing the hallway outside the patient wards, all I could think of was how he'd never been able to stand up to Ma.

Before I could stop myself, I said, "You can't keep letting this happen."

At first he stared back at me; then, he leaned in close. "You've been back for a week," he said, face red with the effort of keeping his voice low. "You don't know anything."

I tried again. "Maybe I should talk to her."

"Who's stopping you?" he asked.

When I didn't respond, he smoothed his shirt into his waistband. "I'm going downstairs to get a drink. Want anything?"

For an instant, I thought he was referring to a bar, but then I realized he meant the hospital canteen. These days Ba rarely touched alcohol. Even though I hadn't consumed anything all day except cereal, the thought of eating made my stomach churn. "No, thanks," I said.

He didn't try to change my mind. He just turned and walked to the elevators.

"Ba," I called, wanting to tell him that maybe I would join him for dinner after all.

Without looking back, he raised his hand in a half wave and kept going.

Standing before the door to my mother's room, I drew my face to the window. There she was, propped up on two pillows, thinner and frailer than she'd looked the day before. An IV needle pierced her left arm, and PVC bags hung off the side of the bed, their tubes leading to places I didn't want to think about.

My mother had always been slender, but she'd lost weight over the last year. Her cheeks were yellow and waxen, as if formed from a synthetic material intended to mimic real skin. After enduring months of hair loss, she'd ordered her longtime hairstylist to "get rid of it all," and her once long, glossy locks now hung limp at her chin. Despite these setbacks, she refused to act like someone who spent her days moving from bedroom to hospital to bedroom again. Each morning she donned the graphic print silk blouse and pressed slacks and stack of real gold bangles that had been her teaching uniform. Even today, clad in a standard-issue hospital gown, the slash of candy-apple red on Ma's mouth looked freshly applied. Some days, I admired her uncompromising standards; other days, I pitied her.

Although an issue of *The Economist* lay tented over her chest, she was staring at the mounted television screen, where a bubbly, perfectly coiffed, blond woman — America's favorite daytime talk show host — urged viewers to, "Stop saying 'no,' and start saying 'Hell, yeah!'" The studio audience of middle-aged housewives burst into ecstatic whoops. Sturdy and wide eyed, these women possessed a wholesomeness I associated with the Midwest, but the show was taped in San Francisco. The host's Pac Heights mansion was a popular sight on city architectural tours.

When she heard my knock, Ma hastily clicked off the TV.

"My long lost daughter," she said. "I have to be lying in a hospital bed before I get to see you."

I busied myself with pulling up a chair.

"Where do you go after work?" she asked. "Where are you spending all your time?"

These were fair questions. I'd spent the last two nights by myself in Holland Village at Chaplin's, a shabby bar with torn leather stools and an empty patch of dance floor that was nothing like the heaving, undulating place I remembered from summer breaks, back when the smoke had been so thick, you lit up in self-defense.

I said, "How are you feeling?"

She scowled. "That Dr. Yeoh. He keeps telling me to eat more, but then in the same breath he says, 'No salt, chili, sugar, garlic.'" She ticked the list off on her fingers. "What am I supposed to eat? And your father. He takes everything so seriously. He was sitting there, taking notes as if he'd forget. I told him, 'Just write, *nothing with taste.*'" She looked pleased when I cracked a smile. "Seriously though, with all this dialysis, what does it matter what I eat? And does Dr. Yeoh not realize that I live with the soy sauce king of Singapore?"

Alcohol was absent from the doctor's list of banned ingredients; I suspected this was Ma's own omission. Given how I'd spent the previous nights, ordering one vodka soda after another to delay having to step through the doorway of my parents' home, I was in no position to judge.

"Ma, we have to talk about this," I said, placing a hand on her forearm, searching for a way to show her I understood.

"Oh, don't start, ducky. I feel fine. I told them I didn't need to stay overnight, but of course, no one listens to me."

I interrupted. "How many did you have?"

She looked away.

I told her that once she got home we would sit down and devise a plan. Perhaps it was time to return to the manuscript she'd all but abandoned, a biography of the germanophone African writer, Dualla Misipo. "You can't just sit around all day," I said.

She pursed her candy-apple lips. "Really? Because everyone keeps telling me how sick I am, and that's what sick people do."

I wouldn't let her draw me in. "I'll give you piano lessons."

She stopped short. She'd always wanted to learn to play, but had never had the time. "Oh, Gretch," she began.

"I'm very strict. I'm used to dealing with eight-year-olds with ADD." As part of my masters program, I'd volunteered at a public school in the Richmond.

She laughed weakly.

"Good," I said. "We'll start right away." I thought of my father in the hospital cafeteria, sipping from a can of artificially flavored apple juice, and wished I hadn't been so harsh.

Ma took my hand. "There's something else I want to discuss."

Beneath my fingers, her skin felt parchment-paper thin. I fought the urge to let go.

"Did Paul reach you at work?" she asked.

I couldn't help but pull away. "Why were you talking to him? What did he say to you?" Then I caught myself. "Why are we even getting into this right now?"

"What exactly happened between you two? Why won't anyone give me a straight answer?"

"I think we have enough to discuss right now," I said. "Like why you're sucking down gin and tonics in the middle of the afternoon."

Her eyebrows came together in the center of her forehead and just as quickly separated. I'd finally said the words, and now I had no idea what was supposed to come next.

A loud beep shattered the silence: the IV infusion machine. A nurse bustled in without knocking and silenced the beeping. "Everybody doing fine?" she asked. She inspected the needle in Ma's elbow crease and rotated her forearm in the air. She didn't appear to notice that neither Ma nor I had answered her question. "I'll be back in an hour to take your vitals," she said and left.

I wished I had some reason to call the nurse back. I was afraid to look at Ma's face.

She spoke first. "You are thirty years old," she said. "It's time to start acting your age. Your problems won't disappear simply because you want them to."

I stood with such force that my chair tipped over and landed on

36

its back with a metallic clang. "Right. You would know. You're a wonderful example of how to face problems head on."

"Don't talk to me like that."

"Like what?" I yelled.

"Sooner or later you'll have to tell me what's going on. Why not start now before you lose him for good?"

"Fine," I said. "You want me to talk? I'll talk. And when that's out of the way, maybe we can focus on why you're in the hospital. Because your drinking problem seems to be the real issue here. You're turning into a drunk." The word rang in my ears. I didn't know if I was finally saying all the things that needed to be said, or if I was trying to avoid talking about Paul. But even in my heated state, I sensed that telling Ma about the affair would unleash a slew of other issues I wasn't ready to examine. Once I started talking, there would be no taking any of it back.

She said, "He can only forgive you so many times."

It took me a second to realize she thought I was to blame. I stood there with my lips parted, trying to figure out where to begin.

Ma let out a sigh. "Come," she said. "Sit."

Before she could say anything else, I hurried out the door and down the hallway, past my tired, confused father. "Where are you going?" he asked.

I shook my head and told him I'd be home later and pounded the button to close the elevator door.

In the parking lot, I dug in my purse for my phone and scrolled through the list of missed calls, watching the curser jump back to the beginning to highlight Paul's name. I twisted the knob on the radio and scanned the channels until I caught the opening notes of

Dvořák's New World Symphony. The blazing sounds of brass instruments filled the car.

I was five when I first heard the slow, stately melody of the second movement on my mother's record player. Afterward, I'd gone over to the piano and plucked out the horn solo, right on key. When my mother—eyes feverish with excitement—described the moment to my piano teacher, my teacher agreed that I must have perfect pitch. Ma loved to recount that old story; I couldn't remember the last time I'd made her so proud.

I switched back to the soft-rock station and drove out of the parking lot. As I waited for the light to change, I considered going back to Chaplin's. The bartender was a balding Englishman who only charged me for every second drink, but picturing his watery eyes and down-turned mouth made me even more depressed than I already was. Instead of veering west to Chaplin's, I got on the Pan Island Expressway to avoid rush-hour traffic, and before I knew it, I was heading back in the direction of the factory.

Two stoplights ahead of Lin's, I swerved into the parking lot of Jalan Besult Hawker Center. I told myself that my colleagues probably wouldn't even be there anymore, but if they were, I'd just stop for a quick drink. Surely no one would mind. Surely they'd be friendlier outside the office.

The hawker center was a large, open-air hall that housed four dozen independently owned food stalls, each specializing in a single signature dish, from barbecued stingray coated in fiery, pungent shrimp paste to Hokkien *mee,* a mixture of yellow and rice noodles, fried with eggs and then braised in rich, savory prawn stock. At this hour, the hawker center teemed with couples on their way home from work and families who lived in the nearby government-subsidized housing estate. The air smelled of wok-fried garlic and the cleaning chemicals doused on tiled floors that never completely dried in the humidity.

As I weaved my way through the tables, I sensed scrutiny of my soft leather bag, of my intricately embroidered black-and-white blouse and slim pencil skirt.

The beer stall was on the opposite end of the hawker center, where Fiona, Shuting, and Jason were squeezed around a table alongside four teenage boys in white short-sleeved shirts and khaki shorts — the uniform of a well-regarded secondary school. Shuting noticed me first. Her eyes grew large. She lowered her head and muttered to the other two. Surprise, then panic spread across their faces, and I knew I'd made a colossal mistake.

"Hi," I called out, waving enthusiastically. What else could I do?

They mumbled hello back.

The teenagers looked up briefly and then returned to their steaming bowls of noodles.

"Want to sit down?" Fiona asked weakly. She tried to slide over on the bench, creating a sliver of space.

Shuting's eyes narrowed. "How's your mum? Everything *eh sai boh?*"

"She's fine," I lied in that same loud, bright voice. I told them I couldn't stay, I was just picking up dinner to bring home — although all of us knew there was no way I would have driven back here.

"See you Monday," I cried, before hurrying around a corner, past a hawker carrying a stack of bright green plates, who scowled and shouted at me to watch where I was going.

Giggles erupted behind me — giggles that I knew belonged, in part, to Fiona, Shuting, and Jason. I could already imagine the pitying looks and barely concealed snickers I'd receive at work.

Back inside the car, I cursed my own stupidity. I wished I hadn't stormed out of the hospital. I even considered returning to apologize. But I was so tired of Ma's constant disapproval. She didn't understand why I couldn't pick a career and stick with it, why after getting a master's degree in English, I now needed one in music education, why I'd given up on my marriage, why I'd let my father talk me into working at Lin's.

My mother believed her best years were the ones she'd spent as a doctoral student at Cornell. From the very beginning, she was determined to prepare me for a life away from Singapore: She named me after her favorite Schubert *lied* even though she knew everyone here would stumble over the name. She convinced my father to send me, their only child, halfway around the globe to boarding school in California. Later, when I was in college and my parents first met Paul, she counseled Ba not to immediately dismiss my *ang mo* boyfriend.

After all she'd done to set me free, here I was, right back where I'd begun.

The car was hot and stuffy and the backs of my thighs stuck to the leather seat. I rolled down the window and sat there with my hands on the steering wheel until the lights came on in the parking lot. Then I reached for my cell phone and called Paul.

It rang once, twice, three times before I realized it was the middle of the night in San Francisco. I was about to end the call when he answered.

"Why, hello there," he said, his voice gruffer than usual.

I stumbled over my apology, wondering if that girl was right there beside him in bed.

"Calm down," he said, giving that low throaty chuckle that got me every time. "I'm at work. You didn't wake me."

So he was still pulling all-nighters like a college kid. A computer science postdoc at Berkeley, he'd always said there was something magical about working until the sun came up.

I tried to relax. "Why did you call so many times?"

Paul said, "Well, listen, I was going to send you a convoluted email, but decided it'd be quicker if I called. Then I couldn't remember which number was for your cell and which was for your parents' house, and then your mom said to call you at work." He rambled when he was tired.

"Okay," I said, drawing out the last syllable.

He said the couple subletting our apartment was selling weed out of the living room. Neighbors—probably Mrs. O'Donley—had complained, and the landlord was giving them until the end of the month to move out. "If it's okay with you. I think we should split the remaining rent and be done with it."

My throat tightened. I didn't know if I was about to laugh or choke. This was what he'd needed to discuss? This was what had prompted him to call all over Singapore looking for me? I started to cough and reached for the half-empty bottle of water in the passenger seat of my car.

Meanwhile, Paul was explaining how much time and hassle we'd save by not bothering with new subletters—another noisy, happy couple traipsing across our apartment's creaky, sun-warmed wood floors, ooing at the bay windows that looked out on the Golden Gate Bridge.

Suddenly it struck me that this was his problem. He'd created this mess in the first place, and he could figure out how to deal with it.

When he told me that my half of the rent came to twenty-seven hundred dollars, I said, "Actually you owe my dad money. Take my share out of that." Five years earlier, my mother had insisted that my father pay off the rest of Paul's college loans as part of our wedding gift.

"Oh," he said.

I knew he was coloring in the letters on a phone bill or credit card application or some other sheet of scrap paper, the shading growing darker and more frantic as he thought of a response. This was a guy who refused to take cabs in the pouring rain, who preferred sleeping in turtleneck sweaters to running up the heating bill. He'd hated taking the money in the first place.

"I'm going to pay him back," he said. "I just need some time. You know what I'm making as a postdoc."

I said, "Maybe you should have thought this through before moving out." What a relief it was to finally say those words.

In a steady voice he said, "This may be hard for you to understand. Most of us don't have over five thousand dollars sitting in the bank."

His words sliced through me. "Maybe your girlfriend can help you out. Oh, wait, she's an undergrad."

"Leave her out of this," he said in a menacing tone I hadn't thought him capable of.

What had I expected him to say? That as a matter of fact they were no longer happy together? That she was gone? I pounded a fist against the steering wheel and accidentally sounded the horn. Its beep was a short, sharp slap. At the end of this conversation, Paul would get in his car and drive home and crawl into a bed already warmed by that sleeping girl. At the end of this conversation, where would I be?

He exhaled long and slow. "Let's not be this way."

Jamming my forehead into my palm, I tried to tap into the white-hot anger I'd felt moments before, but found only dead ash.

"Where do I send the check?" I asked.

He gave me his new address, 62 Lowell Street, and I tried not to picture his new apartment in the Berkeley Hills. Didn't wonder where he'd placed our coffee table, fashioned from an abandoned door we'd found leaning against a dumpster, or the battered love-seat I told him wasn't worth taking, its black velour faded to a dingy green. Didn't wonder about what kind of bed he'd bought after we'd agreed—the only thing we'd agreed on—to junk our old one. Didn't wonder whether they slept beneath one large comforter, or whether he'd insisted, right away, that they each have their own.

"Is that it?" I asked when I'd written everything down.

"Gretch," he said in a voice that made my breath catch in my throat.

I waited for him to go on, but then he thanked me and hung up.

3

FROM TIME TO TIME during our last year together, Paul's computer science research assistant came up in conversation. Her name was Sue, but he called her "the kid." As in, "The kid was coding for me today and wouldn't shut up about that ridiculous new reality show," or, "The kid and her friends are all crazy about that girl band. Kitty Cat? Hello Kitty? It's the worst thing I've ever heard." From hit songs to viral YouTube clips to Internet memes, he became an expert on all things college students were into, but I figured he was just trying to stay connected to his youth. After all, I, too, was feeling anxious about turning thirty.

Five months before the dreaded birthday, I was taking a break from writing my final music theory pedagogy paper of the semester. I don't know what inspired me to type Paul's name into a search engine, but there he was on a site that allowed students to rate their instructors. His page listed his name, the introductory class he taught at Berkeley, and a single posting: "Pretty cool dude, but flirts with female students. Especially a certain cute one." In the kitchen the microwave dinged; I scraped my bowl of oatmeal down the garbage disposal, too sick to my stomach to eat.

Later that night, I pushed my pasta around my plate while Paul recounted the debate he and his officemate had gotten into over the best dive bar in San Francisco.

"The 500 Club," he said, rolling his eyes and making a guttural sound of disgust.

I tried to keep my tone light. "Was Sue there, too?"

"Hmmm?" he said, as if he hadn't heard me.

My fork clattered to my plate.

I wouldn't bring up her name again until a month later, when we were visiting his family in Southern California for New Year's Eve. At six minutes to midnight, I walked into the guest bathroom and found him whispering into his cell phone. While everyone else gathered in the den to count down the last seconds of the year with the crowd in Times Square, Paul and I screamed at each other upstairs.

At first he claimed he was checking his voicemail. But when I held the phone right up to his face and told him to read me the name of the person he'd just hung up on, he snatched back the phone. He told me he could call whomever he wanted; he didn't need my permission; he couldn't talk to me when I was this hysterical. But when I yelled that she was a goddamned child, all the color left his face. He backed away until he stumbled against the sink. The phone tumbled out of his hand and landed in the toilet with a sturdy plop.

"Goddamn it," he yelled so loudly I expected my in-laws to pound on the door.

That night he slept on the futon. We didn't say a single word to each other through the entire seven-hour drive north. Back in San

Francisco, however, he begged me to forgive him and swore he'd never slept with Sue. He said he loved me. He vowed to do whatever it took to earn back my trust.

Unsure of what to do, I turned to Frankie, my old college roommate. That rainy afternoon, she and I sat on a damp bench overlooking the bay, clutching paper cups of coffee.

"He says he's sorry, and I want to believe him."

Frankie frowned and squeezed me arm. She hesitated before opening her mouth. "I don't know, Gretch. I'm not sure I'd ever be able to trust him again."

It was the kind of advice she'd given me countless times before, and yet this time—because I wanted so badly to believe that Paul and I were still a team, because I'd already made up my mind—I seized on the fact that Frankie had never had a boyfriend. Before I could stop myself, I said, "Oh yeah? When was the last time you went on a date?"

Frankie stiffened and looked away, but not before I caught the dismay on her face.

"I'm sorry," I began, but didn't know how to go on.

"Forget it," she said. She tossed her empty cup at the mouth of the trash can, and it slid right in. "I'm sure you'll have no trouble figuring things out on your own."

I vowed to tell no one else about the affair.

For the rest of January, at least, Paul did his best to earn my forgiveness. He hired a new research assistant. He called in the middle of the day to say hi. He surprised me with a weekend trip to Carmel. And I believed he was sincere. The girl was an undergrad. How far could this have gone? Female enrollment in computer science was notoriously low; I'd seen some of them on campus—thin girls in thick sweaters with pale, stringy hair and round glasses worn without the slightest trace of irony.

In February, our schedules filled up with work and school, and we settled back in our normal, separate routines. Paul's paper deadline loomed, and he spent more time at his office, at the library, in coffee shops. He did his best work late at night, so he'd be fast asleep when I woke to go to the gym and then to school. By April, we were so rarely together we were barely speaking. When we both happened to be awake and in the same room, we bickered, or worse, had full-fledged fights about silly inconsequential things: the way he left his dirty clothes in a ball at the foot of the bed, how I forgot to clear my hair from the shower drain.

In May, when he finally told me he couldn't do this anymore, I wasn't entirely stunned, but it didn't hurt any less.

"It's Sue, isn't it?" I said.

His bags were already piled by the door. He looked down at his feet and whispered he was sorry.

I fell on to the sofa, waiting for him to sit down beside me, maybe take my hand.

He shrugged on his backpack. "I'll get out of your way."

Three days after he left, my closest friends at the conservatory convinced me to see the school therapist.

I told the therapist Paul hated how I went from project to project, giving up and moving on when it stopped being fun. "He said getting my second master's degree was mental masturbation."

The therapist nodded and jotted down notes. "And how do you see it?" she asked. "Is music education your passion?"

I started to laugh. Was she serious? Did anyone over the age of eighteen believe in finding one's passion? I said, "I like it well enough."

"Mmmm," she said. Her mouth contorted as she stifled a yawn.

And how about you, I thought, is your passion listening to people whine about how much their lives suck?

I told her my father was the only person I knew who actually loved his work. "He still secretly hopes I'll come home and join the family business."

"And your mother?"

I shrugged. "She wants me to live happily ever after in America, land of the free."

"Has that ever been a source of conflict?" the therapist asked. "Your parents' opposing desires?"

"For me?" I said. "For them?"

"Why does your father hold back? Why doesn't he simply tell you what he wants for you?"

Her tone rubbed me the wrong way. "You'd have to ask him that," I said.

She raised her eyebrows and gave me a tight smile, and I hated her for sitting there with that smug expression on her face.

I said, "Look, I really just wanted to talk about Paul."

But our time was up. The therapist told me to come back the following week, when we could really bite into some of these issues. She smacked her lips together, as if my issues were a big, juicy steak.

Outside, the sun was in free fall and a chilly wind whipped my hair around my cheeks. I tucked my hands in opposite armpits and wandered down Van Ness to the opera house, settling on the bone-cold front steps with my forehead on my knees. Then I was on my cell phone, dialing Paul's number again and again.

"What, Gretch?" he said wearily but not unkindly. "What's up?"

"Why?" I shouted into the phone. "Why her?" I ran up the steps and ducked behind a pillar to shield myself from the wind.

"Where are you?" he asked. "I can barely hear you."

"Why her?" I screamed.

A long pause, and then, "I can't do this again. I'm sorry. I just can't."

When I didn't respond, he said, "I have to go. I'm putting down the phone, okay? I'm hanging up right now."

That night, I lay in bed, unable to sleep. We'd been married for five years, together for twelve. We'd been a couple since before Sue hit puberty. How could he have nothing more to say?

In the morning, I awoke with one arm flung across my eyes, blocking out the diagonal beams of light that shone through blinds I'd forgotten to shut. I stumbled to the living room. The Golden Gate Bridge stretched across the glittering bay, as if someone had laid it down solely for me, but I turned away. My husband was slipping through my fingers, and the only thing I could do was clench my fists and hang on.

With renewed energy, I brushed my teeth and dressed and took BART into Berkeley. It was almost midday, yet students in sweatshirts and plaid pajama pants staggered bleary eyed around the quad. The sun warmed the back of my neck and the California poppies bloomed gold, and all the dazzling spring brightness made me want to take one of those groggy undergrads by the shoulders and shake her awake.

As I headed up the hill to Paul's building, my heart started to pound. I no longer knew why I was here. What would happen when I saw him? Would we hug? Cry? Would he offer to buy me a latte at Joe's? I had no time to ponder the answers to these questions because there, standing in front of the sleek, gray building with his back to me, flanked by a pair of lush potted palms, was Paul—tall, shaggy Paul, in his plaid shirt and ratty jeans, with the addition of one unfamiliar accessory: the arms of a tangle-haired, mini-skirted girl draped around him like a scarf. Arms that belonged to an Asian girl.

Sue spotted me first. Her eyes narrowed as she whispered in Paul's ear. He whirled around, and then turned back to her and said something I couldn't hear. When she took a step forward, he reached for her arm, but she shook free and kept coming toward me with her chin raised.

"Hi," she said, giving me a wide smile and sticking out her hand. "You must be Gretchen." She was a stick figure of a girl, cheerful and bubbly as an anime cartoon.

Paul slapped his palm over his eyes. "Sue," he pleaded. "Let me handle this."

But she ignored him. "We're all adults here. We can be civil to each other."

Blood pounded in my ears. Unable to speak, I gave that girl the coldest, hardest look I could muster. I stuffed my hands deep in my pockets and stepped around her, truly believing that if I could just get to my husband, I could make him comprehend what he was giving up.

But Paul was fixated on Sue. "Please," he said. "We'll talk later. Back at home."

That word was a stone hurled with full force at my gut.

"Promise?" Sue asked sweetly.

Paul's officemate strode past us to the front door. He started to raise his hand, but then his eyes widened as he recognized first Sue, then me. He lowered his gaze and hurried in the building.

Paul closed his eyes and threw back his head. I hadn't seen him this distressed since the night I told him I still didn't feel ready to have kids.

Sue got in a bright red Jetta parked by the curb, and he waited until she'd driven off before turning his attention back to me.

"She's Asian?" Of all the questions I could have asked, this was the first one that popped in my head. Because even after seeing Sue standing there, right in front of me, I still couldn't believe I hadn't known. Paul took a step closer to me, and I placed both palms flat on his chest and pushed. "Sue is Asian?" I repeated.

"Shhhh," he said, looking around furtively.

Adrenaline coursed through my veins. "How could you not tell me?" My hands formed fists that pounded against him. He had lied to me again and again, yet I could not believe that he had withheld this. Suddenly the fact that Sue was Asian was more important than anything else.

"Stop, please." Paul grabbed my wrists. "For Christ's sake, I'm at work."

I let out a high, screechy noise, halfway between a laugh and a wail. "Now you're worried about being professional? Because it's so professional to fuck your assistant? Your undergraduate research assistant?" I didn't recognize my own voice. When had I become one of those women on reality TV, the ones who were always knocking back cocktails and howling in one another's faces?

Paul held up both hands in a gesture of surrender, but I wasn't ready to back down.

I said, "This Susan must be something else. Now you're going to tell me she's mature for her age, right? Wise beyond her years?"

"Sumiko," he said softly.

"What?"

"Her full name is Sumiko."

I released that same crazed laugh. "Do her friends think you're a creepy old man? With an Asian fetish?" As I said the words, I realized I'd never before thought of Paul in this way. I was the first Asian girl he'd ever dated—a fact I'd revealed to my Asian girl-friends with pride. All of us knew or had even gone out with the kind of white guy who spoke Japanese or Mandarin, majored in East Asian studies in college, trained in karate or jujitsu or kendo, and most of all, had a string of Asian lovers in his past. A guy with an Asian fetish was a red flag or a deal breaker, depending on whom you asked, akin to someone who talked with his mouth full, or had mild yet persistent BO.

"Gretchen," Paul said. "Why are you here?"

The laughter emptied out of me. I felt as if I'd had too much to drink and had to sort through endless layers of my mind for the answer.

"Why am I here?" I said finally, throwing my hands in the air. "I guess I'm a glutton for punishment."

"I'm sorry," he said. "I don't know what else to say."

"Did she know I was Asian?" I asked.

Paul sighed. "Come on, Gretch."

I watched him standing there with that weary expression on his face and thought about what I would give to be able to feel the way he did: tired and irritated and ready to move on, instead of helpless, desperate, uncontrollably angry. I took a step forward, and for a split second imagined throwing my arms around him, pulling him close, inhaling his salty, masculine scent.

Instead I shoved him as hard as I could.

He fell back against one of the large potted palms, crying out as the base of his skull struck the lip of the pot, which groaned against the concrete walkway.

I stared in horror and wonder at what I'd done.

"Jesus," he said, gasping to catch his breath. Slumped against that pot, he scowled up at me. "Don't just stand there. Help me."

I turned to go. He didn't need my help.

4

THE FRANKIE SHEPHERD I'D KNOWN for years was a plain, bookish girl who hid the soft folds of her body beneath shapeless sweatshirts and baggy jeans. Frankie's best physical feature, a dimple-framed smile, was too often shielded by the curtain of dark blond hair that swung forward whenever she ducked her head—a gesture that could indicate both discomfort and pleasure. Awkward and earnest, she possessed a clamorous, almost honking laugh that never failed to set me at ease.

The first day of freshman year, in our cramped Stanford dorm room, she touched a warm, clammy hand to mine and aimed her words down the bib of her overalls. I could barely hear her over the noise of beds getting lofted in adjacent rooms and furniture being hauled up the stairs. "What was that?" I asked several times over the course of our conversation, trying to hide my impatience. "Come again?" Already I was thinking about how to introduce myself to the girls next door.

I soon found I'd misjudged Frankie. Once we warmed up to each other, I learned she had a wicked sense of humor and was a gifted mimic. Her impressions of professors were legendary on our hallway, as was her luminous singing voice. That fall, we spent many a Friday afternoon at the music building, working our way through Frankie's impressive collection of musical theater anthologies. I was more than happy to put Chopin on hold so I could accompany her on the piano.

In the winter, Paul and I started dating. We grew used to sharing his extra-long twin bed. Although Frankie accused me of treating our room as storage space, she and I remained roommates the following year. Having been there from the start, she continued to serve as my chief relationship advisor, offering her opinion on such issues as whether Paul and I should stay together through our summer apart, or how to improve his relationship with my father, regardless of her own inexperience, and the fact that she'd never truly warmed to Paul.

Following graduation, Frankie and I both settled in the Bay Area. She later gained admission to Berkeley's Haas School of Business, and it was during this period that she spent a summer interning at the Singapore office of an American consulting firm.

Her first week on the job, she called me long-distance to marvel at the way the locals spoke, how their English took on a tonal, chant-like quality that confused her more than if they were speaking a different language altogether. Singlish, Singapore's unofficial national tongue, combines a singular accent with an idiosyncratic syntax and the blithe incorporation of Chinese, Malay, and Tamil slang words. Frankie said it was as if the entire region conversed in opera libretti in place of regular speech, and given her talent for impressions, she was soon speaking Singlish herself.

Weekends she spent diving in Tioman and trekking in northern Vietnam and suntanning on the white-sand beaches of Bali and Phuket. But it was Singapore she fell for, with all of its paradoxes: its riotous language and spicy colorful cuisine, coupled with its button-downed Confucian values; its pulsing nightclubs and endless government-sponsored self-improvement campaigns. Frankie loved the island's shiny cosmopolitan veneer, as well as its deeply conservative core. At the end of the summer, when the consulting firm offered her a permanent position in Singapore, she accepted at once, only to have her offer rescinded months later due to downsizing. As a last resort, I put her in touch with my uncle, who hired her based on my glowing recommendation and a single phone conversation.

And now, due to the chain of unfortunate events that had played out on my side, here we both were in Singapore. Given my co-workers' continued animosity toward me, I was glad I'd have an ally in Frankie.

The day after her plane touched down, Frankie called to ask how we'd be celebrating her first Saturday night in town. Although she'd spent close to twenty-four hours in transit, she sounded cheerful and energetic and not at all jet-lagged. In contrast, my own voice was thin and hoarse from disuse. I'd been lying awake on top of my old pink floral bedspread for the better part of the last hour, too restless to fall asleep, too weary to get up.

"You sound tired," Frankie said. She lowered her voice. "Is everything all right?"

The tension drained from me like water from a sieve. If she'd been standing before me, I would have thrown my arms around her. For once there was no need to pretend. I told her that aside from work, I'd spent the last week in virtual solitude, ignoring emails and phone calls from friends who'd heard I was back. These were people I'd known all my life, the children of my parents' friends who, like me, had gone abroad to England and the US for college and graduate school. Unlike me, however, they'd returned home to become lawyers, investment bankers, and entrepreneurs, to marry secondary-school sweethearts and live in downtown condos purchased by parents as wedding gifts. By now they all knew about my separation, my mother's kidney failure, my cousin's disaster. If ever my loneliness got the better of me, imagining their solemn faces and voices thick with concern reminded me to keep my distance. It felt good to be able to say all this. Even though seven months had passed since Frankie and I had last seen each other — I'd been busy trying to save my marriage, she'd been busy searching for a new job — I knew she understood.

"You have me now, so you can stop moping around," she said, laughing to show she meant well. "You're going to be so sick of me by the time you go back to school."

Frankie suggested a quieter activity, something just the two of us. "Maybe we could go to the movies," she offered, but her disappointment was palpable.

"Absolutely not," I said. I told her I was taking her to a party, and not just any party, but Kat Tan's thirtieth birthday party, held at her parents' District 10 mansion, despite the fact that she and her husband had long since moved out. I'd never replied to Kat's email — I hadn't even spoken to my old friend since my return — and up until the moment I extended the invitation to Frankie, I'd gone back and forth on whether to attend.

Frankie was talking so loudly I had to hold the phone away from my ear. As always, her energy was infectious. Soon I was digging through the suitcase I hadn't bothered to unpack for my makeup bag, scanning my closet, now partly filled with Ma's unused cocktail dresses, for something to wear. I told Frankie I'd come by to pick her up.

That evening, I flagged a taxi and headed to Frankie's new apartment on Coronation Road, a mid-rise, avant-garde monstrosity of rose-colored tiles that resembled a 1970s-style bathroom. The taxi idled at the curb. I was inspecting my lipstick in a pocket-sized mirror when a fist rapped on the window.

The mirror flew into my lap. I pushed open the door with such force I almost knocked her over. Frankie had mentioned she'd lost some weight over the past couple of months, but she had to be a good fifty pounds lighter.

"How could you not tell me?" I asked.

Frankie ducked her head but she was smiling. "It's not like it happened all at once."

I could not stop staring. Undulating curves and soft, rounded edges had given way to sharp angles, steep planes. Frankie's hair was pulled back in a neat ponytail that highlighted the diagonal slope of her cheekbones, the long unbroken line of her clavicles. Most surprising of all were the child-sized wrists I held in each hand. Prior to this moment, I would never have believed that someone who had been so large could have such tiny bones.

The taxi driver honked the horn. "'Scue me, miss," he called. "This loading zone, *hor*. Cannot just wait here."

Frankie elbowed me in the ribs. "Escue me," she whispered in Singlish.

"Don't," I warned, but I was already cracking up.

In the backseat of the taxi, Frankie told me about her flight and her new sublet. Each time I glanced over, her appearance shocked me once again.

The taxi turned down a narrow, tree-lined street flanked by overgrown houses that strained the limits of their respective plots. In a country so dense that eighty percent of the population lived in government-built high-rises, no amount of money could buy space that simply didn't exist.

Kat's house was different. Even with its high steel gate and phalanx of imported palm trees, its elegance was evident from the street. The Tan family had flown in a famous Beverly Hills architect to design the sleek, two-story, all-white cube, which had been profiled in two local society magazines. The other side of the house, I told Frankie, was even more impressive, with floor-to-ceiling glass windows overlooking a vanishing-edge swimming pool, surrounded by fragrant frangipani trees and hedges of fuchsia bougainvilleas.

I was still groping in my purse for my wallet when Frankie reached over me to hand the driver a ten-dollar bill. "Thanks, uncle. Keep the change," she said. When she caught the incredulous look on my face, she shrugged and said, "What? I spent three whole months here, you know?"

Standing at the gate, Frankie gazed up at the house and let out a low whistle, but I was too nervous to respond. I couldn't recall the last time I'd come to a party like this without Paul. During our short trips back to Singapore, he and I had always embraced our outsider status. We gawked like tourists at my childhood friends, marveling at the insularity of their lives, taking comfort in the knowledge that we were different. In contrast, Frankie was ready to dive into her new life. Her eyes were alert, her posture erect. Even the air around her seemed to shimmer.

In front of the door, I lay a hand on Frankie's shoulder, hoping to coax some of her positive energy up through my palm.

"Ready?" she asked.

I turned the doorknob and watched the door swing open.

Inside, the house was filled with people dressed in varying interpretations of the party's "Roaring Twenties" theme—chosen to commemorate the end of Kat's own roaring twenties. There were a couple of flapper dresses and Louise Brooks wigs, but the majority of the crowd was simply dressed up: girls in sequins, guys in blazers and jeans. They spilled out of the living room and onto the patio and garden surrounding the swimming pool; they clustered around the outdoor bar and the long table laden with finger foods: dumplings in bamboo steamer baskets, assorted sushi rolls, chicken satay made onsite by a hired cook—a wizened Malay man who'd brought his own mini grill and pandan-leaf fan. All around us, people laughed and hugged and talked in frenzied voices over the ambient trance music streaming from surround-sound speakers.

"I'm way underdressed," Frankie said, anxiety shading her face for the first time. She smoothed her black tank top over the waistband of her jeans and undid her ponytail.

"You look fine," I said, pleased that at the last minute I'd abandoned trying to look like I didn't care, and changed into a silk top that hung from the thinnest of spaghetti straps.

Frankie didn't need to be told to kick off her sandals and nudge them next to the other pairs lined up by the door, as I did with my heels. Stalling for time, I paused before the hallway mirror to check for mascara smudges. Frankie joined me, combing her fingers through her hair, and the sight of our reflections gave me another jolt. All at once, my cheeks seemed too full, my jaw-line too prominent, everything about me too short and squat.

I turned away from the mirror. "Shall we?"

"I guess," she said, tugging again at the hem of her top.

My envy faded. "You look great," I said.

She nodded but seemed unconvinced.

At the far end of the living room, the birthday girl stood by the bar in a sparkly tiara and a dress made from tiers of silver fringe. In one opera-gloved hand she carried a long cigarette holder with an unlit cigarette; in the other, an enormous bouquet of orange tulips. I'd been so focused on myself, I'd forgotten to bring a gift.

"*Zar boh,*" Kat cried when she spotted me. She thrust the tulips at her husband Ming and hurried over. "Where the hell have you been? Why haven't you returned my calls? My own mother had to tell me you were back in town." She scanned the length of Frankie's new body before refocusing on me. "You're lucky there are too many people around for me to wring your neck."

I tried to laugh away her words. "It's great to see you," I said. I didn't blame Kat for being upset. She was the only Singaporean friend I'd kept in touch with through my years abroad, and I'd done a lousy job of it these past months. When Paul moved out, I'd emailed her the news, and then had failed to respond to her increasingly frantic messages.

Kat wrapped a satin-encased arm around Frankie. They'd met once before during Frankie's first visit to Singapore. "Welcome back," Kat said evenly.

I could tell she was trying to decide whether to mention Frankie's weight loss. She was about to say more when a tall, well-built man, his face already flushed, backed into her.

"Hello, watch where you're going, you big oaf," Kat said, only half kidding.

The red-faced man found his balance. "Sorry, my dear," he said with a gallant bow.

Shaking her head in mild disapproval, Kat explained that he was her husband's army *kaki*, a friend from his mandatory military service days.

He was already taking Frankie's hand. "Hello. I don't believe we've met."

Frankie blushed and ducked her head, and for an instant, with her newly chiseled face hidden, she was my college roommate again—the girl I had to beg one of Paul's friends to take to the Screw-Your-Roommate dance, and whom he promptly abandoned on the dance floor for the skinny redhead who lived above us. That evening, I left Paul with his boorish friends, and she and I, still clad in our strapless dresses, biked downtown for a late-night ice cream cone.

"*Aiyah*, Seng Loong, get out of here," Kat said, playfully shoving the red-faced man. She led Frankie and me to the bar where she handed us each a champagne flute. "Ming," she called to her husband. "Look who's here. And come meet Frankie."

Unlike his wife, who floated about the room, waving her cigarette holder as if it were a natural extension of her arm, Ming shuffled over in the three-quarter-length dinner jacket and high-waist trousers that Kat must have picked out. A bead of perspiration trickled down the side of his face, and half of his dapper little moustache had come unglued and now dangled limply by his mouth. Ming was small and bug-eyed and had always looked slightly stunned behind the thick glasses he'd traded for contacts after he met Kat. When they first started dating, Paul and I placed bets on how long they'd last.

Now I hugged Ming and told him how great it was to see him. I was about to introduce Frankie when we heard a loud pop. The trans music–spewing speakers snapped off, and a series of *arpeggios* rose from the back corner of the room. At the grand piano sat a short, bald man in a three-piece charcoal-gray suit. He inhaled dramatically before breaking into a flashy rendition of "Smoke Gets in Your Eyes," filled with improvised trills and *glissandos*. The dim lights glinted off his clean-shaven pate, and I recognized the classmate with whom I'd once performed a four-hands piano duet at our primary school's National Day concert.

"We should have Gretch take a turn," said Frankie.

"We should," Kat agreed.

"That's right," said Ming. "I forgot you played."

"Maybe after a few drinks," I said to shut them up. Even though my old piano still stood in my parents' living room, I hadn't touched a keyboard since I'd sold my Steinway upright to a classmate last month — for extra cheap because she let me stack boxes of music books in her basement storage unit. The one thing I did bring home was the bulky, old-fashioned, wooden pyramid of a metronome I'd owned since college, but it sat forlornly on my night table, reduced to a large, impractical paperweight.

The pianist played on, each verse more ornate than the last. Lyrics filled my head: *They said someday you'll find / all who love are blind / Oh, when your heart's on fire / You must realize / Smoke gets in your eyes.*

As the piece came to a close, the pianist segued niftily into something from *West Side Story*. Two girls clutching at least a dozen silver heart-shaped balloons squeezed past us. They were dressed almost identically in slinky halter tops and tight black pants.

"Happy birthday, Kat!" they chimed in unison, unclenching their fists.

The balloons shot up in the air. The crowd let loose a chorus of "ooooo's" and "ahhhh's." One enthusiastic guest started to sing "Happy Birthday," and then his voice trailed off when no one else joined in. The pianist played on without missing a beat.

Kat said, "Those two are too much."

"Where are we?" Frankie whispered in my ear. "*The Great Gatsby?*"

Somewhere nearby a girl screamed with laughter.

I took Frankie's wrist and wondered when its slightness would stop surprising me. "Let's go outside."

Before I could step though the patio doors, Kat's hand clamped down on my forearm. "Give us one minute," she said to Frankie as she dragged me to a corner.

"What? What did I do?" I said, trying to sound jovial.

She folded her arms across her chest and studied me. "How are you?" she asked, managing to turn the question into an accusation. When I opened my mouth, she said, "No, really. How are you?"

"I'm doing great."

Kat's eyes narrowed. She took my face between her palms and pulled me so close our noses almost touched. "I never liked him, you hear me? He was never good enough for you."

I jerked away, stunned by how instinctively I still rushed to defend Paul. I nodded, unable to speak.

"Okay," she said, releasing me. "Go have fun."

Still choked up, I backed away.

Outside by the bar, the red-faced man had already tracked down Frankie.

"I didn't get a chance to properly introduce myself," he was saying. "I'm Seng Loong. I also go by Pierre." He flashed two rows of yellow teeth.

I almost laughed out loud, but Frankie tucked a strand of hair behind her ear and smiled shyly. "Hi, Pierre. I'm Francesca."

She never used her full name.

"Francesca. Are you Italian?"

She nodded. "On my mother's side."

Neither appeared to notice as I stepped away to refill my empty champagne flute and cram a plate with as many sticks of satay and sushi rolls as it could hold. I retreated to the far side of the pool, away from the lights and the people.

From my new vantage point, I watched Pierre tell Frankie a story, the climax of which involved him getting down on all fours and crawling around her in a circle. She threw back her head and laughed with her throat stretched long, her hair a shimmering sheet of gold.

It was as though Frankie had shed her former self like a heavy coat. What had she done with the solid, sturdy girl I'd seen only seven months earlier, the afternoon she'd urged me to give up on Paul? Recalling my obnoxious response to her advice, I felt her dismay and humiliation afresh. And yet, how many admirers had she accumulated since then? What new insights into love had she gained?

I felt a tap on my shoulder and whirled around so quickly the champagne flew from my glass.

"Good thing I brought you a refill." There, standing before me, champagne flute in one hand, Heineken in the other, ridiculous fauxhawk and all, was James Santoso.

"What's a nice man like you doing at a debauched affair like this?" I set my empty glass on the ground and accepted his full one.

He pointed to the red-faced Casanova, who had cornered another hapless girl by the buffet, and explained that he and Pierre were former business school classmates. "So you see, I came with the most debauched of them all."

I scanned the patio for Frankie, and figured she must have gone inside. Meanwhile, James was eying my full plate. He pointed at the little dish of soy sauce in its center. "Ms. Lin, you are the last person I expected to find out here, dipping anything in that swill they pass off for soy sauce."

I shrugged. "Haven't you ever craved a really greasy slice of pizza? Or popcorn drenched in that awful synthetic butter?"

His mouth twisted in mock disgust. "Never," he said. "I don't know about you, but I eat only organic, all-natural, whole foods."

I picked up a sushi roll with my fingers and made a big show of dunking it in the sauce before popping it in my mouth.

James clicked his tongue against his upper teeth. "The horror, the horror."

When I finished chewing, I said, "The trick is to hold your breath."

He let out a big laugh, and I felt the stress seep out of me.

Across the pool, guests swirled about like schools of colorful fish.

He followed my gaze. "Do you know any of the one million people at this party?"

As a matter of fact, I did. Over there, seated on a deck chair, was Cindy Lau, my childhood second-best friend. When we were nine, Kat, Cindy and I had purchased identical fake-gold, heart-shaped pendants, inscribed with the words BEST FRIENDS. We'd vowed to wear them forever — except I kept accidentally wearing mine in the shower until all I had left was an illegible black lump of oxidized brass. Beside Cindy was her husband Terrance, who spent most of his time at the Island Country Club, lifting weights and playing tennis while his wife worked long hours as a corporate lawyer. That tall, skinny girl with the purple feather boa was Liwen Poon, who I heard had given up her venture capital job to release an album of pop songs. Coming through the patio door was Mark de Souza, the boy every girl in my primary-three class had had a crush on, and beside him, with her hand in the back pocket of his jeans, was his current girlfriend Lakshmi, a former computer programmer turned restaurateur.

"So if you know everyone, why are you out here all by yourself?" James held my gaze, a wry smile on his lips.

Something about his expression or his American accent made me think, *Maybe I could try to explain, maybe he would get it.* Out of the corner of my eye, I caught Frankie making her way over, and disappointment poured through me.

She said, "I've been looking all over for you."

"How'd it go with Pierre?" I asked.

"So, you're the one he was going on and on about," said James.

I introduced James and Frankie to each other, explaining that he was Lin's newest client and that she was about to be Lin's newest employee.

"So you moved all the way here to pursue your love of artisanal soy sauce?" he asked.

"Not quite," said Frankie. "I moved all the way here to pursue my love of Singapore, though I'm more than willing to get acquainted with artisanal soy sauce, too."

I watched them exchange grins.

From across the pool Kat called my name. She was waving her arms and crying that I couldn't possibly be planning to hide out here all night. I shot Frankie and James an apologetic look.

"Don't worry about us," James said. "I'll give Frankie a crash course in the art of soy sauce brewing."

I followed Kat inside.

The crowd in the living room had thinned. My childhood duet partner was still at the piano, and a group had gathered around to sing a Mandarin ballad I didn't know.

"Drinks off the piano, please," Kat said as we swept past.

The silver balloons had spread across the ceiling like an ominous pattern on a weather map. Occasionally their thin black ribbons brushed the tops of guests' heads, causing them to look up in alarm. Kat approached the group lounging on the circular couch, and I trailed behind.

"And so I told him, if I'm going to give up coffee, you better do it, too," Cindy was saying. She pecked Terrance's cheek and laid her head on his shoulder.

"It's true," he said. "That first week, she *kena* caffeine withdrawal, I didn't dare take breakfast with her."

"Just be glad you're still allowed to drink champagne," said Cindy. She turned to me. "Gretch. Finally decided to show your face."

Only the slightest mound of a belly protruded from beneath her slim red dress, but I'd already heard the news. "Congratulations!" I said, straining to imagine how it would feel to inhabit a body that was no longer solely mine. Out of nowhere the weight of Paul's accusatory stare bore down upon me. *You don't have that much time.*

I assured my friends that I was doing well and happy to be home, and they tactfully refrained from questioning me further. When Ming appeared with a tray, I gratefully accepted another drink. After that the conversation turned to the group's annual Bali trip, the wedding they'd attended the month before, the bar in Robertson Quay opened by a mutual friend. At first I listened intently, trying to visualize the people and places they mentioned. But soon I gave up. I gulped down the rest of my champagne. Perhaps it was time to collect Frankie and go home.

The pianist and his off-key chorus reached the end of their song. When the group had dispersed, the pianist started up again, this time with the opening broken chords of an aria from *Phantom of the Opera*.

Two bars in, a high, clear voice floated in the air, silencing the room.

"Think of me, think of me fondly, when we've said goooood-bye." There was Frankie, perched on the piano bench. Face serene, eyelids at half-mast, she sang the words from memory in that silvery soprano I remembered so well.

Glasses froze in midair; canapés congealed on plates; punch lines went unsaid. Terrence put his arm around Cindy and stroked her belly with his free hand. For once Kat looked genuinely impressed, and she caught my eye and mouthed the words, "Oh my God."

The old Frankie would have never gotten up before a room full of strangers, no matter how tipsy she was. The new Frankie acted like it was no big deal. There was an insouciance to her performance, a hint of a shrug—as if she understood she had an obligation to share her gift. Indeed, her voice had acquired a new suppleness, a sparkling coquetry enhanced by flashing eyes that were all the more prominent in her narrow face. My thoughts drifted to the legendary opera singer Maria Callas, whose dramatic weight loss was said to have caused the decline of her voice. What kind of desperation drove someone to swallow a tapeworm?

When Frankie reached the end of the song, her final note hung suspended in the air. The entire room erupted. Someone cried for an encore. Others called out requests.

Frankie ducked her head, brushed off the compliments and disappeared into the kitchen.

"Your friend is so lovely," said Cindy.

"So talented," said Terrence.

"So pretty," said Lakshmi.

All around me, everyone was talking about the beautiful *ang mo* girl with the enchanting voice.

Truthfully, I was proud to have Frankie by my side. Her performance had finally made me understand her affection for my homeland. Here, in Singapore, she was novel, exotic, something of a curiosity. But instead of increasing Frankie's self-consciousness, the attention was liberating. Forced to engage and entertain, she could try on different personas; she could be confident, gregarious, relaxed—all the things she wasn't back in America.

After a while, the pianist and the two identically dressed girls who had brought the balloons came around to rally the remaining guests to go out dancing.

"I have my car," slurred one of the girls as she leaned on her twin to hold herself up.

I went to find Frankie.

From beyond the kitchen door, I heard her exuberant, honking laugh. "There she is, the star of the moment," I said, pushing open the door.

She was sitting on the counter, her long legs dangling against a cabinet. "Hi, Gretch," she called out.

"Hey, hi," said James.

My gaze moved from one beaming face to another. I wondered how long they'd been hanging out here, alone. The pianist barged in to inform us that everyone was going to Zouk, and we had to come, too; the cabs were on their way.

"What's Zouk?" Frankie asked.

"What's Zouk?" the pianist repeated in exaggerated disbelief. "What's Zouk?" He took her arm and led her out of the kitchen as he explained why Zouk was the greatest nightclub in all of Singapore—in the world, even—and he wasn't kidding when he said he'd seen a lot of nightclubs.

James was still leaning against the kitchen table with his arms folded. "Are you going?" he asked.

"Are you?" I stifled a yawn.

The smile spread across his face in slow motion, like honey over bread. "Why not?"

"I guess someone needs to keep an eye on Frankie."

Neither of us moved. I was close enough to smell his cologne—something velvety and expensive.

"Let's go," he said, straightening. He placed a hand on the back of my neck and gently steered me to the door. His palm was warm and smooth, the pressure reassuring. When we joined the others in the foyer, he let his hand fall, and I missed its weight.

At half past midnight, three taxis pulled up in front of a large converted warehouse on the Singapore River, and twelve revelers in flapper dresses and tail coats, tiaras and top hats, tumbled out. It was drizzling—a soft spattering of drops so different from the icy San Francisco rain that pricked like tiny needles on your skin. But it was Saturday night, and the line of people determined to dance until dawn snaked around the side of the building.

Frankie, James, and I followed our friends to the front of the line. At the club's entrance, the pianist exchanged high fives with the bouncer, and the two identically dressed girls waved their VIP cards like winning lottery tickets. The bouncer unclipped the velvet rope and nodded us through, and three girls at the head of the line caught my eye. Barely eighteen, defiantly thin in mini skirts and tube tops, the girls watched our group with such raw envy that I saw us through their eyes: carefree and buoyant, old enough to do whatever we wanted, young enough to be responsible only for ourselves. Remembering how it felt to want so badly to be someone else, I had an almost maternal yearning to warn the girls against being fooled by appearances.

Inside the club, violet light rained onto the dance floor where hordes of people gyrated to a thumping base so loud every cell in my body pulsed in time. I resisted the urge to clamp my hands over my ears. Paul, the self-proclaimed dive-bar connoisseur, would have turned and walked out the door. James, however, looked unfazed. When he caught me watching, he closed his eyes and shimmied his shoulders and crooned along.

The thumping base gave way to a Zouk standard, an old Belinda Carlisle song, updated for the twenty-first century with wailing synthesizers and a frenetic beat. On the dance floor, the crowd sang and moved in unison, like the chorus line of a Broadway musical—a peculiar Zouk trademark that seemed to embody the mindset of an entire nation: even inebriated, at our most free, we all chose to mimic each other.

As we climbed the stairs to the VIP balcony, Frankie shouted over her shoulder, "How the hell does everyone know the same dance?"

"Repeat clientele," James shouted back.

"Empowered conformity," my mother would have said in her postcolonial-scholar voice.

A knot formed deep in my abdomen. Ma had returned home from the hospital earlier in the day, and so far, I'd managed to avoid being alone with her. Tomorrow, I promised myself, I would stop hiding. Tomorrow, I would do all the things a good daughter would do.

My friends and I settled around a table far enough away from the speakers to be able to converse by shouting in each other's ears. A waitress delivered pitchers of vodka and cranberry juice with a fistful of straws in lieu of individual glasses, and I filled my mouth with the syrupy stuff, hoping the additional alcohol would somehow fend off the ache spreading through my skull. Was this how my mother drank? Because she'd rather step off the edge into darkness than spend another second rooted to the same spot?

When a new song with a salsa beat came on, the pianist and the two girls leapt up. They danced their way to the edge of the balcony so they could lean over the railing and wave their arms in time. Across the table from me, Ming pulled Kat to her feet. Mark and Lakshmi followed, then Cindy and Terrence. I reached for the pitcher and drank.

The pianist turned back and beckoned for Frankie and James and me to join them. I shook my head, but wasn't surprised when Frankie tossed back her hair and let out a piercing whoop.

James shot me a sidelong glance.

The throbbing had crept around to my temples. "You should go," I said.

"I'm going to need a couple more drinks if we have to listen to this crap all night." He tipped the pitcher toward him, took one sip and scrunched up his face. "I haven't had anything this bad since I was a fourteen-year-old girl."

In spite of myself I giggled. He winked at me and went to join the others.

Alone at the table, I looped my bag on my arm and mapped out my path to the staircase, trying to gauge whether I'd be able to slip away without anyone noticing.

A moment later, Frankie was by my side, dabbing a piece of Kleenex to her sweaty forehead. "But we just got here," she said.

"Stay. You can catch a cab. Kat will make sure you get home."

Her face tensed with concern. "I'm coming with you." When I objected again, she said, "Gretchen, I've slept a total of seven hours in the last two days. I'm coming with you."

While Frankie waited in line for the restroom, I waved hastily at my friends, hoping to escape without a fuss. Only Kat came over to say good-bye. "Don't be a stranger," she ordered. "And definitely bring Frankie out again. She's the best."

"Isn't she?" I said. A remix of an eighties dance hit came on — another song I'd first heard at this club over a decade earlier. Suddenly I felt impossibly tired, impossibly old.

At the head of the stairs, James was leaning on the banister, swigging a beer. "Bedtime?" he said.

"Listen," I heard myself say. "If you're in town for a while, maybe we could grab a drink sometime?" The question reverberated in my head; I didn't think I'd ever spoken those words. I was glad it was too crowded for any of my friends to observe this interaction.

Seconds ticked by. And then he hooked his thumb beneath my chin and waited until I met his gaze. "Okay," he said. "I'd like that."

I gave him my number, and then I hurried down the stairs to Frankie who was waiting by the door, bobbing her head to the beat, entirely oblivious to what I'd dared to do.

Outside, the rain had ceased and the air was a soggy sponge. Frankie and I slid into a taxi, a boxy royal-blue Toyota that reeked of synthetic floral air freshener. Chinese pop music blared on the stereo, drowning out the ringing in my ears but not my thumping heartbeat. I slumped back in my seat and tried to calm down.

Frankie reached her arms skyward and gave herself a good stretch.

"Did you have fun?" I asked.

"I had a blast." She placed her fingertips on my forearm. "How about you?"

"A blast," I agreed, though with each passing second, I could feel my mortification swell inside me

The taxi hurtled away from the river and down a side street lined with brightly lit twenty-four-hour eateries that catered to the ravenous post-clubbing crowd. I counted parked cars to make myself stop thinking about James.

Frankie rested her head on the windowpane, closed her eyes and let out a satisfied sigh. "This is going to be an amazing year," she mumbled, barely audible over the radio. Her jet lag had finally caught up with her. "I'm really happy we're together, in the same place."

She didn't appear to expect a response. In the moonlight her skin was ghostly pale, her face placid as a lake. I imagined my own face in sleep, my sullen mouth and creased brow.

When the taxi neared Frankie's pink-tiled building, I nudged her awake. She yawned and thanked me for bringing her along and wrapped her thin arms around me in a big hug.

"See you on Monday," I said brightly, even though the thought of facing Shuting and Fiona filled me with dread.

"First day of work," she sang back. She got out of the cab, pushed open the glass doors to her building and disappeared into an elevator.

When I turned back, the cab driver was eyeing me in the rearview mirror, waiting to be told where to go.

"Queen Astrid Park, please," I yelled over the bubblegum harmonies of a Mandopop girl band.

The driver shouted back, "Nice area. You just visiting? You not from Singapore?"

I switched to Singlish. "No, *lah,* uncle. I'm Singaporean. I just move back. From States."

Perhaps not completely convinced, the driver switched from English to Chinese. "You still can speak Chinese?"

"*Hao jiu mei yong,*" I answered. It's been a while.

"Good you haven't forgotten," he said. "My kids' Chinese is very poor."

"Young people," I said.

"Young people," he agreed.

Leaning back, I took in the lights streaming past my window, the tourists still drinking pitchers of sangria at sidewalk bars. I tried to picture myself with James at one of those tables, and the image made me cringe. He probably wouldn't call anyway, and if he did, I could make up an excuse.

The taxi turned off the main road, and the stately, colonial-style houses of my parents' neighborhood came into view. As we wound our way through silent streets, I let my eyelids shut, and this time I saw Paul.

We were sitting at his parents' dinner table in Irvine, California. His father was telling this loud awful story, with lots of fist pounding and fork waving, and his mother and brother and sister all screamed with laughter. But I just sat there, smiling blankly, unable to concentrate, because Paul had my hand under the table, and with his index finger in my palm, he spelled out, "I love you," over and over again.

The taxi approached the gate. My parents' house loomed on the hill, with its Spanish red-tile roof and ornate wrought-iron balconies, and even in the darkness, its opulence embarrassed me. I rummaged through my purse before giving the driver a twenty-percent tip, which he, thinking I'd miscounted, tried to hand back as change.

5

AFTER A DAY SPENT MOPING around the house, pretending not to be waiting for my phone to ring, I awoke on Monday morning determined to put the events of Saturday night behind me. I told myself I needed to make the most of my remaining time here in Singapore. So, instead of lying in bed with the covers over my head, waiting for Ba's car to pull out of the driveway, I showered, dressed, and hurried downstairs, stopping in front of my mother at the dining table.

She lowered her newspaper and looked up expectantly, revealing the stray breadcrumbs on her chin. I wanted to reach out and wipe them away. "I have to go to work now, but I'll be home for dinner. I'll see you then?"

She blinked rapidly and glanced over at my father who was standing by the front door. "Of course, ducky. Where else would I be?"

Ba was rifling through his briefcase, pretending not to observe my exchange with Ma.

I told him he was right; it didn't make sense to drive separate cars to work.

He zipped shut the briefcase, cracked the knuckles of both hands, and said, "Come. Let's go." To Ma, he said, "We'll see you tonight."

On the Pan Island Expressway, as the Mercedes crawled along in rush-hour traffic, Ba and I listened to the morning news on the classical music station, delivered by a local newscaster in a fluty British accent. Headlines included the rise in bicycle theft on the island's eastern side, the arrest of a Swedish couple who'd streaked down a main road on a Saturday night, and the launch of the government's annual "Speak Good English" campaign to discourage the use of Singlish. The things that constituted news in this country always amused me, but today I was too preoccupied to make jokes.

Outside my window, the boxy bungalows gave way to modern condominiums like Frankie's, then to towering public housing developments painted cheery shades of lemon, lavender, mint. I waited for the broadcast to end before turning down the volume. "Ba, there's something I want to talk to you about."

His eyes flicked up to the rearview mirror and back to the road. "Yes?"

"Since I'm only going to be at Lin's for a few months, I'd like to do more than just administrative stuff. Maybe I can work on something actually related to soy sauce?"

His face brightened. He gave the steering wheel a jaunty slap and wagged his index finger at me. "I told Ma you'd come around."

I smiled back, determined to do whatever it took to avoid having to work with Fiona and Shuting, even if it meant assuming more responsibility at the company.

Ba took his eyes off the road for an instant and looked straight at me. "Xiao Xi, I'm proud of you."

I swallowed my guilt. It pained me that something this small could give him such joy.

Ba had kept quiet when I chose not to major in business or economics in college. He protested much less than my mother when I decided to go back to graduate school to study music education. Chinese parents typically inserted themselves into every aspect of their children's lives, but not Ba. Having interpreted his silence to mean he just wanted me to be happy, I'd felt lucky to have him.

Now, taking in Ba's gleeful expression, I realized that what I'd always read as contentedness was simply an indifference toward any choice I made that didn't involve working at Lin's. If I wasn't going to join the family business, he really didn't care how I spent my time.

My father grew serious. "Actually-*ah*, there is something Uncle Robert and I need help with. Something you'd be perfect for." He paused as though to build suspense.

I asked what it was.

"We need someone to take over the US Expansion Project."

The US Expansion Project was Lin's largest growth opportunity and Cal's pet cause. It dawned on me that at some point over the weekend, Ba and Uncle Robert had reached a resolution.

"What's happening to Cal?" I asked.

This time, Ba kept his eyes on the road. "He's gone."

"What do you mean gone?" I said. "Is he back in the Maldives? When is he coming back?"

Ba squinted up at the roof of the car as if searching for answers. "Cal no longer works for Lin's."

I couldn't believe his words, and the lack of emotion behind them. My cousin was the only one among us grandchildren who'd shown any interest in the company. And he was the oldest grandchild, the sole boy.

"And Uncle Robert agrees?" I asked.

"No choice, *lah*," Ba said. "He has to agree."

His cavalier attitude stunned me. I'd expected Ba and Uncle Robert to reprimand Cal one more time. I'd expected them to insist that he run all future decisions, big and small, by them before he made a move. I never thought firing my cousin was an option.

When I pressed Ba to explain his decision, his fingers tightened around the steering wheel until his knuckles turned white. "What Cal did was unacceptable. I don't care who he is, he cannot stay."

No matter how I tried, I could not imagine Uncle Robert firing his own son. I couldn't even imagine my stoic father going through with the plan. Ba and Cal had grown close during my early teens, around the time when I'd refused to sit through any more of my father's tastings. Back in those days, he'd invite Cal to the house every time he wanted to test a new product or sample a competitor's sauce. He and Cal spent hours debating the quality of sauces the way others discussed their favorite sports teams. They devised a complicated ranking system and recorded the results on hand-drawn charts that my father still had. If ever I felt the slightest tug of jealousy, I needed only to remind myself that as long as Ba had Cal, I was free to do whatever I pleased. As far as I could tell, Cal's sisters, Rose and Lily had taken a similar approach; both of them had recently chosen full-time motherhood over careers.

My next question seemed so absurd I almost didn't ask. "Who's going to run Lin's if not Cal?"

My father grew very still. "Xiao Xi, Cal does not understand why Ahkong founded this company. I would rather give up everything than leave Lin's to him."

The air around us seemed to thicken. I fumbled with the air-conditioning controls.

In the adjacent lane, a small pigtailed girl pressed her face to the car window and stuck out her tongue at me. I checked if Ba had noticed, but he stared straight ahead. He took the next exit, pulled into the factory parking lot and killed the ignition. For a while he was silent; then, as we walked up the stairs, he said, "Don't worry, *lah*. I'll take care of this. You only need to focus on two things: spending time with Ma, and learning what you can while you're here at Lin's."

The enormity of the US Expansion Project dawned on me. Suddenly my increased responsibilities weren't so appealing, after all. I followed Ba into his office. "Hang on," I said, pausing to shut the door. "I'm not sure I can do this. I'm nowhere near qualified."

A hint of a smile played in the corners of Ba's mouth. "You know more than you think. You've been around soy sauce your whole life."

When I continued to object, his patience thinned. "*Aiyah*, I'll be here. Uncle Robert will be here." He thought for a moment. "And if Frankie is as diligent as she was in college, she'll help, too."

"Put Frankie in charge," I said. "I'll be her assistant." I pointed out that Frankie had a fancy business degree. She knew all about consumer research and emerging markets and product positioning. I paused, trying to come up with more business terms. "You remember she used to be a management consultant, right?"

Ba cupped one hand in the other and cracked his knuckles extra loud, causing me to cringe. "But what does she know about soy sauce?"

I opened my mouth, unwilling to admit defeat, and when nothing came out, Ba pounded his desk in triumph. "*Han-ah*. Get to work."

On my way out, he stopped me. "Your uncle will make the announcement. Until then, please-*ah*, not a word."

I assured him I could keep a secret.

Before I closed the door, I turned. "What will you do if Cal won't leave?"

He looked baffled. "This is a family business, not the WWF."

His joke made me laugh, but I wasn't so sure.

I left Ba's office just in time to catch Frankie emerging from the stairwell for her first day of work. Clad in a knee-length shift dress and patent leather peep-toe pumps, her damp hair slicked back in a bun, Frankie gleamed like a showroom car. All activity on the office floor came to a halt. Shuting stopped feeding paper into the shredder despite the machine's insistent whine. Fiona's voice trailed off in midconversation with Jason, who spun around to see what he was missing. In those heels, Frankie towered over the women and most of the men.

"Gretch, hi," she said, oblivious to the stir she'd caused.

I showed Frankie to her office, a room formerly used as a storage closet. In preparation for her arrival, the other admins and I had piled the boxes of documents in one corner, but the closet and shelves still overflowed with stacks of printer paper, spare staplers, and six different models of ballpoint pens.

Frankie insisted she didn't mind. "Interesting choice of paint," she said, taking in the pale-pistachio walls. "Very calming."

"Sorry about all the gawking. You'd think they'd never seen a white person before."

"Oh, it's not so bad," she said.

After I gave her a brief overview of everyone on the office floor — "Avoid the drama vultures in marketing; be nice to Fiona, she has more power than you'd expect" — Frankie and I hunkered down to evaluate the work Cal had already done on the US Expansion Project. Given my cousin's love of shortcuts, his tendency to keep crucial information to himself, and his questionable vision of a more modern Lin's, we were skeptical about whether his recommendations could be trusted.

From the start, I told Frankie she was in charge, and the arrangement seemed to please her. She got to work at once, methodically making her way through Cal's files, hunting down marketing and sales people — and even my father — when I was of no help. If she noticed the way her new colleagues whispered about her American assertiveness, she didn't let it bother her.

In contrast, I treated the work like a college class: doing the minimum it took to get by. I tried to coerce Frankie into taking breaks by showing her hilarious pictures I'd found on the Internet and bombarding her computer with inane instant messages. She'd indulge me for a minute or two before returning to work, but after I emailed her a third cat picture, she spun around to face me and said, "Look, I realize your uncle hired me mostly as a favor to you, but I really think I can make a difference around here."

Duly chastised, I began to read the files she deemed most relevant, and the more I learned, the more I had to admit that some of this stuff was actually interesting. Who knew that specialty food producers from bastions of Americana as Gainesville, Florida, and

Louisville, Kentucky, had begun to experiment with artisanal soy sauce? According to a prominent food magazine, the Kentucky producer even aged its sauce in old bourbon barrels for an added whiff of smoke and local color. Top chefs all over America were raving about the depth of flavor the smoky sauce brought to dry-aged filet mignon and buttery black cod. An avant-garde chef in Chicago had infused the soy sauce into butter. The resulting concoction was spread on bite-sized brioche, topped with tobiko caviar, and served as the *amuse bouche* to his seventeen-course tasting menu.

One didn't need to pore over these files to discern the burgeoning excitement for all things natural and handmade — after all, Frankie and I both hailed from San Francisco, the epicenter of the artisanal food movement. And yet Lin's was edging away from its traditional brewing methods.

I filled Frankie in: several months earlier, Uncle Robert's first move as president had been to purchase the factory's first industrial fiberglass tanks, a decision my father had opposed. To avoid further angering Ba, the tanks had been housed in a shed, away from Ahkong's jars and out of sight. The new additions were large gray-green vats, as different from one of our jars as a Yamaha violin from a Stradivarius. But Uncle Robert argued that each fiberglass tank had five times the capacity of a single jar. Furthermore, the workers would no longer have to hand-stir the fermenting soybeans since a simple twist of a valve would agitate the contents of each tank. As a result, fermentation would be reduced from six months to four, shortening production time and lowering costs.

Frankie tapped her pen on the table. "Makes perfect sense. Especially if it all basically tastes the same, right?"

I didn't hide my incredulousness. "We can't go any further until you try some sauce." I reached over, closed Frankie's laptop and ordered her to move her papers aside.

And so I staged a spontaneous soy sauce tasting right in my office, exactly like the ones I'd seen Ba lead dozens of times. Despite curious looks from co-workers passing by, I made Frankie take one sip after another of our premium sauces, until I was sure she understood the value of our clay jars — jars that were rinsed every six months in tepid water and left to dry in direct sunlight. This special treatment protected fifty years' worth of golden residue that coated the jars' insides and gave our sauce its signature earthiness.

"Incredible," Frankie said, smacking her lips. "I've had plenty of soy sauce in my lifetime, but this sauce isn't even remotely the same species."

In a few weeks, I promised, when this season's batch was fully aged and ready to be strained, I would take her downstairs to inspect the tawny glaze.

When the tasting was over, I mixed two Sprite cocktails and handed one to Frankie. Her face contorted in a wince but when I stared her down, she accepted the glass and took a tiny sip before admitting — as everyone did — that the drink was surprisingly tasty. I told her that when Ahkong really wanted to impress guests, he used to add a couple drops of Tabasco sauce and a lemon wedge — a nod to a classic Bloody Mary. "Next time," I said to Frankie, who was draining her glass.

By the end of the day, we'd done enough research to conclude that consumers were growing more discerning than ever. Despite my uncle and cousin's certainty that customers wanted a less expensive product, it appeared that demand for artisanal soy sauce was on the cusp of taking off. Lin's was moving in the wrong direction. If we proceeded as planned, some other company would swoop in to fill the space we'd left behind.

That evening, Ba and I drove home together, and I had dinner with my parents for the first time in days. The next morning, Frankie and I got back to work, compiling our research into a report to present to my father and uncle. By the time we were done, those same colleagues who'd snickered at Frankie's never-ending questions now spoke reverentially about her work ethic. They no longer paid attention to me.

Frankie and I were so engrossed in our work, I didn't have a chance to reveal my previous interaction with James. Or else I didn't allow myself the chance. Given that the likelihood of his calling dwindled with each passing day, I ordered myself to forget I'd ever asked him out. I only hoped I wouldn't run into him anytime soon.

Near the end of Frankie's first week at Lin's, Kat called to inform me that all the usual people were meeting for drinks; Frankie and I absolutely had to come. If anything, the previous weekend had confirmed how little I had in common with my old friends, but still I agreed, mostly because it was easier than arguing with Kat.

Frankie and I were leaving the office when my cell phone rang a second time. I considered letting the call go to voicemail, then turned away from my friend to answer, simultaneously hoping it was and wasn't him.

With Frankie's eyes boring holes into the back of my head, I tried to keep the conversation as short and as neutral as possible.

"Tonight?" I said. "Like in two hours? What makes you think I don't have other plans?" I knew I should have been offended by the last-minute nature of this call, but I was thrilled to hear James's voice.

"Well, do you have other plans?"

I didn't answer right away. I glanced back over my shoulder at Frankie who was waiting with her hands on her hips, a suspicious look on her face. I went through the motions of weighing my options, then said, "I'll see you at seven."

"Who was that?" Frankie grinned wickedly.

I hurriedly explained how James had obtained my number, and Frankie listened, amused. "If it's so not a big deal, then why'd you keep it a secret?"

I ignored her question. "I'm really sorry I have to bail on you." If I hadn't been so excited about my date, I would have felt guilty about spoiling Frankie's night.

To my surprise, she assured me she was perfectly happy to meet up with my friends on her own. She wrote down directions, entered Kat's number in her phone, and promised she'd do her best to downplay my absence. "Have a good time," she said in a tone weighed down by a string of caveats.

Two hours later, showered and blow-dried, painted and powdered, I was in a taxi speeding toward the restaurant, my ambivalence intensifying with the rate of my pulse. The same thoughts I'd considered and dismissed rose up once again: Did he really expect me to drop what I was doing and rush to meet him, especially after taking five days to call? Why was I doing precisely that?

"Uncle, don't mind turn up air-con can?" I asked the cab driver. I reminded myself to breathe.

James and I were meeting at Clarke Quay, a strip of bars and restaurants on the banks of the Singapore River — our island's most famous river, which was puny enough to be mistaken by tourists for a canal. Back in the nineteenth century, the Clarke Quay area had been a major port, and the government had done its best to preserve that historical charm, albeit in sterilized form. Crumbling godowns had been gutted and given fresh coats of candy-colored paint. Smooth cement boardwalks were laid down around evenly spaced palm trees. An army of neon green-clad workers was on hand to sweep up any traces of litter that had fallen short of the ubiquitous trash cans, themselves sleek and glossy enough to be mistaken for sculpture. Here in Clarke Quay, every table was clogged with local yuppies and Caucasian expats and Australian and Japanese tourists, yet the bars and restaurants turned over each year.

James's pick was a new tapas bar pragmatically called Tapas Bar. The space had formerly housed a seedy bar slash lounge that had gone by the more enigmatic name of China Black. I'd been there once or twice in my twenties — just frequently enough to be able to reference it whenever my friends and I needed an example of what we *didn't* want to do on a Saturday night.

James was already standing outside the restaurant door, immaculately dressed in a periwinkle-blue button-up shirt and jeans so stiff, they had to have been ironed. His fauxhawk had been flattened and artfully tousled. Just as I raised my hand to get his attention, he pulled his phone from his pocket and began tapping on the screen. I pulled back my hand and slowed down, hoping no one had witnessed my awkwardness.

A moment later, he caught sight of me. Before I could hesitate, he came forward and gave me a hug. "Glad you could make it."

I took a step back and waited for him to explain why he'd taken so long to call, and when no explanation came, I said, "It was a challenge to clear my schedule, but I managed."

He laughed like it was the best joke he'd ever heard, then dropped his voice a notch. "By the way, you look amazing."

"Why, thank you," I said extravagantly to mask my pleasure.

"Shall we?" He whisked the door open and motioned me through with a bullfighter's grace, something Paul never did—out of principle, he claimed.

As I stepped into the cool entranceway, the toe of my pump caught the edge of the rug, and I fell forward. I let out a yelp and grabbed onto James with both hands.

"I got you," he said in a low voice.

The muscles in his arm were hard and lean beneath my fingers. I dropped my hands to my sides, startled by the comfort of his touch.

"You okay?" he asked, his gaze locking onto mine.

I brushed my hair away from my face and choked out that I was fine.

A waiter who had caught my gaffe hurried over.

"She's just really excited to try your food," James said.

Tapas Bar's new proprietors had renovated extensively since I'd last visited this location. Gone were the low-hanging lanterns, leopard-print couches and faux sheepskin rugs. The space had been stripped down to its concrete floors and ceiling beams. The restaurant's sole embellishment was an oversized canvas of wild paint splotches that spanned an entire wall.

The waiter led us to a spacious corner table. We were taking our seats when a slender man, his trimness amplified by his narrow pinstriped suit and skinny black tie, materialized before us. "I thought

I saw your name on the list," he said, pumping James's hand. "So good to have you."

James asked how business was, and the slender man waved a hand over the packed dining room and said, "No complaints, no complaints." He instructed us to flag him down if we needed anything. Then he glided down the aisle, nodding and smiling at patrons as he went.

I lifted a questioning eyebrow at James, who shrugged and said, "Restaurant industry. Small world." He opened his menu and fell silent.

I, too, pretended to read while I studied him from across the table. Here was a guy who was comfortable in his own skin and was used to being treated well. He was the antithesis of scruffy, defensive Paul, who dismissed all codes of etiquette as elitist and stiffened in the presence of cloth napkins and weighty silverware. How Paul would have disapproved of this lively, airy room, this impeccably groomed man. I smoothed my napkin over my lap and resolved to enjoy the evening.

James continued to study the menu. When he flipped the page, a small, sapphire-blue sphere glinted in the buttonhole of his French cuff.

"They're not going to quiz you on that later," I said.

He laughed and rubbed a palm across his smooth chin. "Menus are like poetry," he said.

I tilted my head. I couldn't tell if the tugging in the corners of his mouth was the beginning of a smirk or a smile.

He spread the menu on the table. "The way it's structured into smaller sections, the way each line prepares you for the next. Every good menu tells a story: the chef's history, his inspirations, his hopes." He looked up at me expectantly.

"When was the last time you actually read a poem?" I asked.

James pushed aside the menu and laughed.

The waiter appeared carrying a peculiar vessel with an extra-long, narrow spout. "Aperitif on the house," he said. "This is a cava from the Penedès region of Spain. A *brut nature*."

James glanced over to verify I understood, and I felt my spine straighten in indignation. "My favorite kind," I said, though in truth there was something endearing about his concern.

"Super dry, super crisp, and excellent with food," the waiter said, before raising the vessel high above his head and aiming the spout in my glass. The sparkling wine formed a perfect arc that made my mouth water.

"That pitcher is called a *porron*," James said, rolling the *r*'s with gusto. "Traditional Catalonian wine vessel."

I could almost feel the toe of Paul's shoe, nudging me under the table. "Can you believe this shee-shaw?" the look on his face would say. And yet, I knew I would have defended James.

The waiter explained that *porrons* were typically brought out for birthdays, weddings, and other festive occasions. The long spout was designed to be aimed directly into a waiting mouth.

I said, "Very efficient."

"Not to mention environmentally friendly," said James.

The waiter waited for our banter to taper off before asking if we were ready to order.

"You start," I said, scanning the endless list for the first time.

James studied me. "How hungry are you?"

The question felt like a test. "Starving."

"Good. Me, too." He clapped shut his menu. To the waiter he said, "We'll have one of everything."

He had to be kidding. The restaurant served at least thirty different dishes. But James handed his menu to the waiter and waited for me to do the same.

"Hang on, cowboy," I said. "The last time I checked we were ordering for two."

James placed one hand over mine and told me not to worry. The portions would be manageable. "See?" he said pointing at my menu. "*Small* plates."

His palm was as warm and smooth as I remembered. I could still feel its fading imprint on the back of my neck. In spite of myself, I surrendered my menu.

Before long our entire table was covered in food: an earthenware ramekin of pearly-pink prawns bathed in garlic butter; translucent, paper-thin slices of cured ham fanned out on the plate; *tortilla espanola* with nuggets of potato and sweet onion; candy-stripe beets studded with goat cheese and almond slivers; slow-cooked short ribs almost silky in their tenderness; thick chorizo stew.

James ate with great concentration, head lowered, eyes trained on his plate, face flushed. Occasionally he looked up and declared that the beets would benefit from a touch of *fleur de sel*, or that the short ribs were out of this world. I admired his lack of self-consciousness, his unabashed passion. When we weren't discussing the food, we told each other what we missed most about America: greasy-spoon diners, red plastic cups, buying in bulk.

"Good bagels," I said

He closed his eyes and nodded approvingly. "There was this one bagel place by NYU that I used to go to at least three times a week. I still dream of those bagels." His eyes darted open. "But you're from California, so I'm not sure you know what a good bagel tastes like."

"Hey," I warned. But when he laughed, I laughed, too.

Near the end of the meal, after I'd set down my knife and fork, and James had finally pushed away his plate, and we'd ordered espresso in place of dessert, I asked, "So how'd you decide to come back home after business school?"

James dropped a lump of raw sugar in the tiny cup and stirred. "I didn't decide. The choice was already made." The expression on his face was matter-of-fact. He raised the cup to his lips and downed its contents in two long pulls.

I waited for him to go on, but he dabbed his mouth with his napkin as though to indicate there was nothing more to say.

"I guess that makes things easy," I said. "My parents gave me all the choices in the world, and then stood back and let me do whatever I pleased. And look at me now." Our eyes met, and I dropped my gaze, suddenly embarrassed. This was a small town; we had plenty of friends in common. I knew I didn't have to elaborate.

He chuckled softly and said, "You seem to be managing just fine."

When he signaled to the waiter, I felt a pang of disappointment, knowing the evening was about to end. How stupid of me to call attention to my failed marriage. It had been so long since I'd been on a date, I'd apparently lost all ability to carry on a conversation.

Instead of asking for the check, however, James winked and said, "Let's end this meal on a high note." To the waiter, he said, "The lady is ready to try the *porron*."

"No. I don't think so," I said. "Definitely not." But the waiter was already heading to the bar.

When he returned with his pitcher, it seemed everyone in the room had their eyes on me, so I threw up my hands, raised my chin and opened my mouth wide. The cold, tart stream hit the back of my throat as cheers rose from around the dining room. Two tables down, a group of Spanish businessmen burst into song. "*Cumplea-ños feliz, cumpleaños feliz*," they sang, having decided that it was the only logical explanation.

I made it halfway through the song before I had to hold up my hand to tell the waiter to stop. By then, the other tables and the wait staff had joined in in English, as had James, who, in a surprisingly robust baritone, sang louder and more enthusiastically than anyone else.

When the check finally came, I dutifully wrestled for it, even though I knew a guy like him would never let me pay my share. We rose from the table. As we walked out of the restaurant, his finger-tips found the small of my back, sending a jolt up my spine.

The night was breezy and relatively cool. James and I fell in step with each other, and soon we were following the boardwalk along the river. He pointed out where he lived — a trio of tall gray build-ings, not far away, that towered over a dense forest of new luxury condominium complexes. It was nearing ten, and the after-work crowd at the outdoor tables was at its peak: large groups of men, shirtsleeves rolled to the elbows, knocking back mugs of beer; the occasional trio of women who sat clutching their purses in their laps as they eyed the men with equal parts intrigue and revulsion.

James and I strolled away from the shouts and guffaws, the show-boating and posturing, the dense cooking smells, the multicolored Christmas lights draped from rooftops, balconies, lampposts, and more. Here by the river, on this smooth lamp-lit path with the breeze in my hair, my hand slid down James's forearm and landed neatly in his. Hoping it was too dark for him to see me blush, I kept putting one foot in front of the other, but he hung back. Startled,

I spun around. Our arms stretched out between us as though we were in the midst of a choreographed dance. He tugged me gently to him, combing his fingers through my hair as he brought his face to mine. His mouth was warm and wet, his tongue undulating, sly, more alive than any part of Paul. As we sealed the spaces between us, Paul faded from my thoughts, and then I couldn't think at all.

Before long we were in front of James's condo. Through the glass doors, I admired the sparkling marble floors and the pair of art deco chandeliers. Of course he would have a flawless home. Upstairs, I pictured minimalist Danish furniture, sweeping city views.

I said, "Thank you for dinner."

"You're most welcome." He reached out and tucked a strand of hair behind my ear. "I can have the concierge call you a cab."

"Great," I said at the same time that he said, "Unless."

I met his gaze. "Unless what?"

James shifted his weight from one foot to the other. "Unless you want to come upstairs?" He posed the question lightly, as if he were asking whether I took my tea with milk.

I turned the question over in my head.

I hadn't been on a date in over a decade, and I hadn't dated enough in my lifetime to be able to say for certain, but still, I had a feeling that going upstairs was something I wouldn't normally do.

But then I thought about tiptoeing through my parents' dark house and up to my childhood room. I saw myself sitting in bed, scanning the numbers in my cell phone, wishing I had someone to call, someone who would appreciate the absurdity of the position I now found myself in. My exchange with Frankie, while rushed, had been just long enough for her to make clear she disapproved. Kat's reaction would be less measured. I could reach out to Marie or Jenny in San Francisco, but they'd only ever known me in the context of my relationship with Paul. Given that I'd vanished without fully explaining the state of my marriage, the leap to my present circumstances seemed far too vast.

So I tucked my arm into James's, and told him that I would indeed like to come upstairs. Together we walked past the concierge desk to the bank of mirrored elevators at the far end of the lobby, where our reflection caught me by surprise. How symmetrical we looked with our matching black hair, narrow builds, and understated, tailored clothing. We were the kind of couple who appeared in advertisements for sub-zero refrigerators and flat-screened televisions. Paul had towered over me at six foot three; even holding hands had been awkward.

The elevator dinged, we entered, the doors slid shut. As we rose up in the air, I counted the floors—six, seven, eight, nine—wishing I could both stop time and fast-forward to the end.

6

⚘

I N FRONT OF MY PARENTS' HOUSE, I raked my fingers through
unkempt hair and smoothed my rumpled blouse, preparing to
explain where I'd been.

This was uncharted territory. As a teenager, I may have snuck
out to see a boyfriend once or twice, or lied that I was spending the
night at a girlfriend's, but I'd never stayed out without notifying
my parents of my whereabouts. The windowpane by the front door
reflected the ridiculousness of my situation. Here I was, a disheveled
thirty-year-old woman dressed in yesterday's clothes, about to walk
in on Ma and Ba in the middle of breakfast. There was nothing else
to do but get it over with.

When I pushed open the front door, a cry pierced the air—my
mother's—followed by my father's stern retort, too low for me to
decipher.

In the dining room, Cora, my parents' live-in maid, was crouched
low to the ground, broom in hand. When she saw me, she sat back

on her haunches, but clamped her lips together and shook her head. Around her, shards of glass glittered against the marble floor. The jagged lower half of a highball glass lay on its side in the dustpan.

I took the stairs two at a time and found my parents' bedroom door ajar. Ma was on the floor with her legs straight out in front of her, still dressed in her old cotton nightgown, her arms wound tightly around her body.

"I won't," she said, shaking her head so forcefully her lank uncombed hair flopped over her eyes. "I won't, I won't, I won't." With each repetition her voice gained strength.

My father sat on the edge of the bed with his head in his hands. Sensing my presence, he turned abruptly to the door. His face went slack. "Xiao Xi," he said.

I entered the room. "What's going on?"

He gestured to my mother. "Your ma," he said, his voice cracking. He started over. "Your ma isn't feeling well. She wants to stay home, but I'm taking her to dialysis."

My mother struggled to push up onto her knees. I stepped forward to help, but she swatted me away. "She's not a child. Why can't you tell her the truth?" The fermented tang of her breath made me pull back.

"The truth?" Ba said. "Fine. You tell her. You tell your daughter what you just told me."

Ma's lip curled as she spoke. "Don't you try to use her against me. Don't you manipulate me."

"Will someone please tell me what's going on?"

Ba turned back to me. "She didn't want to go," he began.

"Doesn't," my mother snarled in a way I'd never heard before.

"She doesn't want to go. Present tense. *D-O-E-S-N*-apostrophe-*T*!"

Ba didn't flinch. "Your mother says she's done with dialysis."

My gaze traveled from my father's eerily calm face to my mother's, which was frozen in a state of exquisite fury. It had been three months since her kidney failure. Three months since she'd given up work and travel. Three months that she'd spent tethered to that wretched machine for three hours a day, three days a week.

Ba spoke again, "Your ma wants us all to stand back and watch her drink herself to death."

It was the first time I'd ever heard him acknowledge her drinking problem, and I was flooded with relief. Even Ma was so stunned she seemed to forget her anger.

But as my father's words echoed in my mind, panic rose within me. I stepped forward and took my mother's bird-thin arm. Her skin was cold and dry and shifted too loosely over the brittle bone. "Come on, Ma," I said. "You have to go."

"You both think it's so simple," she said wearily.

I could not look at her. I motioned for Ba to take her other arm. "Help me," I said, as though referring to a heavy box, or an unwieldy piece of furniture.

"Careful," she shrieked as he took the arm ridged with the fistula that received the thrice-weekly dialysis needle. But she let us guide her down the stairs.

She said, "I can't spend the rest of my life this way."

And, "What would you do if you were me?"

And, "Are any of you listening? Say something."

Like Ba, I trained my eyes straight ahead. For once, I understood his reticence. Ma didn't need either of us to tell her there were no alternatives to dialysis.

Outside, Ba got in the driver's seat, while I steered my mother to the passenger side of the car. Once I'd buckled her seatbelt, I hesitated with my hand on the door handle. My parents would be at the hospital for the better part of the day. Without an appointment, there was no guarantee we'd get a chance to talk to Ma's doctor. Did I really need to be there?

Ba watched me expectantly; Ma wouldn't glance my way.

"Hold on," I said. "I'll be right back."

He protested that they were running late, but I was already sprinting into the house and up the stairs, past a concerned Cora, who sometimes pointed out the new bottle in the recycling bin, her eyes lowered.

In my parents' bedroom, I pulled a silk blouse from the dozens hanging in the closet, reached for the pair of thin wool slacks draped over a chair, and raced back outside.

Through the car windshield, my parents looked small, vulnerable, and, most of all, old.

I lay the clothes on the back seat of the car. Gasping to catch my breath I said to my mother, "For when you get to the hospital."

She smoothed the cotton nightgown over her thighs and pretended not to care.

"Okay," Ba said. "We really have to go."

I raced around to the other side of the car and hopped in. I hadn't had a chance to shower, but at least James had let me use his spare toothbrush before sending me off with a chaste good-bye kiss that made me wonder if I'd done something wrong.

If Ba and Ma were surprised I'd decided to come along, they

didn't let on. Anchoring a hand on Ma's headrest, Ba backed out of the driveway. He checked for traffic over his left shoulder, and when our eyes met, he smiled.

Once we'd deposited my mother in the dialysis center, I pulled Ba out to the hallway. "When can we talk to Dr. Yeoh?"

He took a step away from me. "We don't need to. She's fine now." He turned to go back in the room. "Besides, it's impossible without an appointment."

"She's nowhere near fine."

A trio of nurses glared at me as they passed. "Please keep your voice down to avoid disturbing the patients," one of them said.

"She's sorry," Ba said sharply.

At the end of the hallway, a door swung open and a young woman in scrubs stepped out, followed by Ma's doctor, a tall man in a white coat with thinning hair and soft jowls.

I hurried toward the pair, calling out the doctor's name.

At first he looked startled, but then he smiled. "Gretchen, Xiong, good to see you. How are things?"

I said, "I know you're busy, but my mother had a really rough morning, do you think we could get your advice?"

The doctor told his colleague he would catch up with her later. "What happened?" he asked.

Before my father could interrupt, I proceeded to recount the events of the morning as quickly as I could.

When I finally stopped to take a breath, I felt Ba's hand on my shoulder. "My daughter just got home. She's scared. And a bit excitable, *lah*."

I shrugged off his hand and shot him a look.

The doctor's eyes passed from Ba's face to mine. He glanced down at his watch and said, "As a matter of fact, I do have a few minutes to chat." He took us to an empty conference room and told us he'd be right back.

"What do you think you're doing?" Ba said.

"Why are you so afraid to ask for help?"

Fuming, we regarded each other across the narrow width of the conference room table.

The doctor returned. "Please, have a seat." He slid a crumpled brochure across the table. "I mentioned this the last time," he said to Ba — a conversation I hadn't been a part of.

The brochure advertised Light on Life, a rehabilitation center that resembled a sun-drenched, tropical resort. Glossy photographs showcased the center's idyllic grounds, but on the back flap of the brochure, a pair of sad eyes peered out of a gray, wrinkled face. Why had they included a close-up of this man who looked so tired, so grim?

I was still staring into the old man's eyes when Ba took the brochure. Barely glancing down, he folded it in half and then in half again. He stuck it in his breast pocket. "We'll think about it."

"Okay then," said the doctor, drumming his fingers on the table in a manner that was too jaunty for the situation and checking his watch again. "And please, really give it some thought this time."

I wanted to reach out and shake the doctor until he told us what to do. Ba and I needed orders, not gentle cajoling. "We will seriously consider it," I said. "Especially because we understand that this could be the only way for her to get better."

The doctor seemed satisfied that he'd done his job. In the meantime, he said, there were things we could keep trying at home:

stricter supervision, more activities, concrete short- and long-term goals. He spouted off the terms as if reading a grocery list. No doubt he saw a steady stream of patients like Ma accompanied by families like ours: in denial, afraid to act.

We thanked the doctor and watched his form recede down the hallway.

Once he was out of hearing distance, Ba said, "It's out of the question." He was already walking off.

I grabbed his arm, but he wrenched away. "This isn't America. We don't ship off family members for other people to take care of."

"This is not the time to be thinking about saving face," I said.

His eyes grew wide; his nostrils flared. He leaned in and took my wrist. "I'm still the head of this household. I get final say."

Only when he let go did I feel the tightness of his grip, the pressure stemming from the tips of all five of his fingers. I knew he wished I hadn't come to the hospital. He and Ma had been a self-contained unit for so long. Xiong and Ling against the world. So much so that I'd been lulled into believing they didn't need me, their only child, that they would always have each other.

He stalked off to the waiting room, and I trailed behind, pausing in the doorway to squint up at the clock on the wall. It would be at least another hour before Ma's dialysis session was over.

Ba settled in a blue padded chair, took off his glasses, and began to work the spot between his eyebrows. I took the chair beside him. "With the right treatment, she can get better."

He returned his glasses to his nose. "If you give people the respect they deserve, they will rise to the occasion."

I fought to tamp down my frustration. "Alcoholism is a disease, Ba."

His voice rose. "We can take better care of her. We can."

After that, neither of us said a word. We sat in silence with our eyes fixed on the door to the treatment rooms, waiting for Ma to emerge, safe and healthy, for at least another day.

That weekend, Frankie called to ask if I wanted to go to the beach with her and Kat and our other friends. "The regular crew," she called them.

A half-dozen snide remarks danced on the tip of my tongue before I isolated the true source of my irritation: to think I was actually jealous that Kat and Frankie had made plans without first consulting me.

"Thanks for the invite, but I'm going to spend the weekend with my mom," I said.

Several hours later, Kat called, too. But when I offered the same explanation, Kat, for once, backed down. "I guess that's a valid excuse," she said. "I'll let you go. Tell Auntie I said hi."

Over the years, I'd spoken candidly to Frankie and Kat about Ma's drinking, though neither of them knew how serious it had become. Given that Ba and I were just figuring out how to deal with Ma's latest developments, I didn't offer my friends any new information, and they didn't ask. They didn't even press for details about my date with James, which disappointed me more than I cared to admit. I was dying to share and analyze every aspect of the date: from how I slept in one of his old T-shirts, threadbare and silky smooth, to the way he kissed the crown of my head in the morning when we said good-bye. Late at night, he'd wrapped his arms around me and pressed my head to his chest, and in this manner we'd fallen asleep. What did it mean that in those last conscious moments, lying there absorbing his strong, steady heartbeat, I felt so grateful I could have cried? What did it mean that when I sent him a text message the following day, it took him six hours to reply? What did it mean that I hadn't heard from him since? I could hear Kat now: "*Aiyah*, woman, what do you expect when it took him five days to phone you in the first place?"

Even if James had called right then to tell me what a wonderful time he'd had, even if he'd wanted to see me again, that very day, I would have declined. I already had plans—plans that could not be canceled. My mother would never say the words, but this time, I knew she needed me by her side.

That Saturday afternoon, while my friends lazed on the beach, I took my place on the bench before the Steinway baby grand that had been my fourteenth-birthday present. It was time for Ma's first real piano lesson.

Twenty years had passed since we'd sat together on this bench. In those days, Ma's role had been half companion, half taskmaster: repeating my teacher's instructions; scolding or encouraging when I complained about aching wrists or general tiredness; fetching me water in a crystal highball glass to match her own.

Through graduate school I'd only ever worked with elementary school-aged kids, and now I wasn't sure how to proceed. "Middle C," I said finally, striking the key, deciding to start at the very beginning.

Ma scowled. "You can't be serious."

I knew she'd picked up the basics from eavesdropping on the lessons I'd started at the age of four. In the beginning, when she'd only worked part-time, she lingered in the dining room grading papers, close enough to absorb everything my teacher said. Together we learned to read notes and made our way through the first two Suzuki Books. Sometimes she put aside her work and joined me at the piano, one of us playing the right-hand line while the other played the left, after which we would switch places and play the piece all over again. But when I got older, she picked up a full course load at the university, and my pieces grew too challenging for her unpracticed fingers. Occasionally, I'd come home from school to find her at the piano, squinting at sheet music as she stumbled through a piece I'd mastered months or even years before. Embarrassed by her ineptitude, I found excuses to leave the room.

On weekends, Ma took me to the Victoria Concert Hall, even though back then the Singapore Symphony Orchestra was a bunch of amateurs—nothing, she said, like the concerts she'd attended in New York, or even Ithaca. Ba served as chauffeur, dropping us off and picking us up. Sometimes he found a parking spot close by and napped in the car—anything to avoid coming inside. Still, after I left for California, I'd expected him to step in and take my place. Instead, Ma went to the symphony by herself a couple of times, and now she didn't go at all.

It struck me that I should buy us tickets while I was home.

Ma was still lamenting how little faith I had in her abilities, but I was determined to continue the lesson on my own terms. I moved on to scales, stressing the importance of learning the correct fingering, reminding her to strike the keys with conviction instead of tapping half-heartedly with her manicured, too-long nails.

She lasted about seven minutes before complaining of boredom, and when I gave an exasperated sigh, she said, "Come now, I'm fifty-eight years old. I don't have time for basics."

I threw up my hands. "Why don't you tell me exactly what you want to learn?"

Ma chuckled and patted my back on that spot directly below the nape of my neck, as she had when I was a small child needing to be soothed. "I thought you'd never ask," she said. "All I want is to play one piece. One beautiful piece. Not even perfectly—believe me, I know my limits—just well enough to be able to play it all the way through without hurting anyone's ears."

I didn't respond right away. An unexpected welling in my throat spread up through the backs of my eyes. It was such a simple request, coming from a woman who had recently lost so much.

"Which piece?" I asked, bracing myself for her answer.

Ma's smile split her face in half. It had been a while since I'd seen those two rows of small, charmingly crooked teeth.

Without hesitation she said, *"Gradus Ad Parnassum,"* and before I could pass judgment, she added, "And don't tell me it's too hard. I'll practice as much as it takes. I have nothing but time."

Her choice shouldn't have surprised me. She loved Debussy, and when she heard me play that piece at my high school senior recital, she told me she'd been moved to tears—a confession that had mortified me. Now, however, twelve years later, I saw she'd meant what she'd said. I nudged Ma off the bench and searched the storage space beneath the bench cushion for the sheet music I hadn't touched since that recital, the photocopied pages still taped together in a single row to minimize flipping.

In truth, it wasn't a bad choice. She could have picked something truly impossible. Although the piece was technically challenging with a couple of crossed-hand passages and tricky key changes, we would start slow.

"Play for me," Ma said.

I didn't see how my performance would get her any closer to her goal, but suddenly my fingers ached to strike the keys. Selling my piano in San Francisco had been a foolish thing to do—an act driven not only by frustration with storage prices, but by my anger at the world for all the terrible, unjust things that had befallen me that month. I wondered if there was any chance Marie would take pity on me and sell me back my piano.

I played *Gradus Ad Parnassum* once through, more slowly than I would have liked, laboring to keep a steady tempo, stumbling a bit on the key change.

"Oof," I said when I was done, shaking out my fingers.

But Ma regarded me fondly, murmuring, "That was lovely, ducky."

I told her to fetch her reading glasses, and she wandered around the living room before declaring she must have left them on her nightstand. I followed her up the stairs, went to my room and came down with my metronome cupped in both hands.

Back at the piano bench, Ma peered at me over her glasses. "You still have that old thing? Surely they make pocket-sized ones these days."

I smoothed my metronome's russet, fine-grained wood. "I like this one," I said. I set the metronome to sixty-six, less than half the tempo listed on the score, and the slow, steady ticking instantly relaxed me. To my mind, a metronome embodied simplicity: once the needle got going, all you had to do was keep time.

"Now it's your turn," I said.

Ma worked her way through the first page at half pace. Every couple of notes, she'd stumble and scowl at the metronome as if it were at fault. "That thing is driving me crazy. How can anyone concentrate over that awful ticking?"

Since it was her very first lesson, I turned off the metronome and let her start over. Already I was starting to reconsider my stance from the doctor's office. Maybe Ba was right; maybe it was too early to consider rehab. Maybe Ma and I could sit here at this piano for a few minutes every day, and it would count for something.

When the lesson was over, Ma went to take a nap, and I settled in the den in front of the television. There again was the bubbly, blond talk show host, Melody.

On this episode, Melody's studio guest was a plump woman with a weak chin and a shoulder-length perm who, in her mid-thirties, already looked like someone who'd once been pretty. The woman, a self-confessed shopaholic, was in the midst of detailing all the ways in which she'd blown through her children's college fund and plunged her family into debt. And yet, despite this woman's horrifying behavior, there was something so naive, so sweet about her confessing all this on television, and trusting that Melody would make things right. No Singaporean would have ever considered displaying her problems to the world, although, judging from the amount Melody was shown on local TV, we clearly enjoyed watching other people do it.

In a halting voice, the shopaholic was recounting how her uncontrolled spending had led her husband to divorce her. The studio audience gasped in horror and sympathy; Melody furrowed her brow and closed her eyes to indicate she was taking in each and every word. When the shopaholic paused to wipe away her tears, Melody enveloped her in a hug. "You are so brave," she said to the now sobbing shopaholic. "You will get better because you are here." The studio audience clapped with all their might.

Even as I dismissed the show, I was pulled in by Melody's plush, sonorous voice, by those gleaming blue eyes that locked on to mine, by the fervor of her studio audience. I too wanted to believe that this shopaholic who had behaved so irresponsibly and hurt so many of her loved ones could be cured. I was so engrossed in the show I didn't even think to change the channel when my mother walked in.

"Oh," she said. "Melody." With one elbow she nudged me over on the loveseat and took her place beside me.

7

M Y MOTHER ALWAYS SAID HER BEST years were spent as a graduate student at Cornell.

"There was so much going on," she'd say, closing her eyes and tilting her head, as if toward some enchanting tune playing in the distance. "Readings, lectures, dinner parties, dances. I worked hard, though. I had to in order to finish my dissertation."

Forgotten Discourse: Toward a Definition of Postcolonial German Literature, a heavy volume contained in a navy-blue cloth binding, sits at the bottom of our bookcase, next to a large leather-bound photo album that holds pictures of my mother from the same period. Younger then than I am now, Ma had waist-length, stick-straight hair that she parted down the middle. She wore fitted cashmere turtlenecks and tweed knee-length skirts and polished high brown boots. She was quite lovely.

Even today, when age and illness have stripped the luster from her skin and the gloss from her hair, my mother's slanting cheekbones and long cat eyes remain unchanged. In fact, without the distractions of youth, her features have become even more striking, like a piece of basswood whittled down to its perfect, essential core.

Stubborn and pragmatic, my mother was a gifted scholar. She carried these traits into her parenting, deciding early on that children should always be told the truth. As such, she never tricked me into believing in Santa Claus or the Tooth Fairy — things I read about in books by Russell Hoban and the Berenstains — though she did dig around in her purse for a shiny gold dollar each time I lost a tooth.

When I asked, at the age of five or six, where babies came from, she thought for a moment and said, "Well, babas have penises. Mamas have vaginas. Right there, where your wee-wee is." She paused to make sure I understood before continuing. "The baba puts his penis in the mama's vagina" — here she formed an O with the thumb and first two fingers on one hand, and inserted her other index finger into the O — "and then the baba shoots his sperm into the mama, which fertilizes her egg and makes a baby."

"But why does he do that?"

She stared off into the distance, thinking. "Because it feels good."

I was not a particularly inquisitive child, so I must have concluded that this was another of those situations in which the answer was significantly less interesting than the question itself, and left it at that.

In primary three, I, along with every other girl in my class, developed a crush on Mark de Souza. Even at age nine he had the wavy brown hair and dimpled chin that, in adulthood, would earn him a place on *Her World* magazine's list of the fifty most eligible bachelors.

Swept away by my feelings for this boy, and newly obsessed with the idea of love, I asked my mother if she'd fallen for Ba at first sight, and she answered truthfully, "No." She said she and Ba had gone out a few times at the end of junior college, but when he made plans to attend the local university, she didn't think twice before accepting admission to Cornell.

Following college, she stayed on in Ithaca for graduate school. Near the end of her doctoral program, Ma began to apply for faculty positions all over the country, but when her parents discovered her plan to remain in America, they begged her to reconsider. Her mother left pleading messages on her answering machine; her father arranged for a dean at the National University of Singapore to interview her over the phone. Their actions only made Ma more determined to build a life away from Singapore.

By then, eight years had passed since my father and mother first dated. Nonetheless, with his future in-laws' encouragement, Ba bought a plane ticket from Singapore to New York City, rented a car and drove the four hours north to Ithaca—all against his own parents' wishes, who couldn't understand why their son refused to forget this strange, willful girl.

Ba appeared at Ma's door the same day her eighth and last job rejection arrived in the mail. The thought of waiting another year and starting the process all over again was too much for her to bear, especially in the face of continued pressure from her parents—and from Ba. By the end of the week, he'd convinced her to buy a plane ticket home to Singapore. She accepted a job at the National University of Singapore, where she was the only faculty member in the humanities department who held an American doctoral degree, not to mention one from the Ivy League. My parents married, and ten months later, I was born.

The tale of how Ba and Ma eventually came together charmed my nine-year-old self. I imagined my father, shivering in a brand-new wool coat, braving the February snow to rescue my mother and bring her home. Only later, after the American visiting professor had come and gone, did I stop to question Ma's choices. If she hadn't loved Ba, why did she come back to Singapore? Did she grow to love him? Did she love him still?

Over time, many of these answers would reveal themselves, and yet the original questions begot others, each more urgent than the one before, a never-ending chain of ever-rising stakes.

The American visiting professor was named Colin Clarke. He had come from the University of Chicago to give a seminar at my mother's university. To welcome him and his wife, the humanities chair hosted a dinner at a seafood restaurant on the eastern coast of the island that was famous for its chili crab.

At first my father tried to get out of attending the dinner. It was no secret that he found Ma's colleagues exhausting. They sat around discussing books he hadn't read, and when he tried to bring up something he'd seen in the paper or on TV, they humored him for a minute or two before taking up the previous topic of conversation. But Ma insisted she could not show up alone. All the other spouses would be there. Eventually, Ba relented, but on the night of the dinner, he announced that I was coming, too. Ma was not pleased.

I had just turned ten, and my opinion of these gatherings fell in-line with my father's. If it hadn't been for the chili crab — plump, succulent mud crabs served in a thick, luscious tomato-and-chili sauce — I would have refused to attend. In between lectures by various faculty members on the history of Singapore cuisine for the benefit of the foreign visitors, Ma and her colleagues discussed their research and their classes. Ba and the other spouses quickly ran out of ways to participate in the conversation, and spent the rest of the dinner nodding and smiling politely. Every once in a while, a grown-up asked me what my favorite subject was in school, or whether I was enjoying the food, but other than that I was left alone.

Colin Clarke's face has faded from my memory, but I can still picture his wife, a frightfully thin woman with pouffy hair the color of pomegranates, who complained about the humidity and the spiciness of the food. She finally agreed to taste a single morsel of crab, then pointedly wiped off her sauce-stained fingers on a disposable towelette.

Only one other aspect of that dinner stuck with me. Near the end of the meal, I noticed Ma and Colin Clarke discussing some writer or philosopher they both admired. Something about the tilt of their shoulders or the angles of their heads caught my attention, and when I glanced back a while later, it was clear from the way they neglected their bowls of honeydew sago that their conversation was far from over. Before I could ponder the heaviness that settled in my limbs, Ba threw back the last of his beer and cleared his throat. He leaned over, looped an arm over Ma's shoulder and questioned them in a loud strident voice about this philosopher of theirs. What startled me was neither his aggressive manner, nor the questions themselves, but the way he spoke. By peppering his speech with phrases like, "No kidding," and "Sure thing," and "You don't say," my father was mimicking an American accent. His eyes glittered feverishly; his face and neck burned bright red. Another colleague tried to engage him in a different discussion, but he would not turn his attention from Ma and the American.

After that, someone — probably the humanities chair — signaled for the check. The academics and their spouses reached for their purses and rose from the table.

In the parking lot, Ma walked briskly to the car, ignoring Ba's comments about the evening. All the way home, Ba continued to speak in that strange voice, and when Ma told him to drop it, he widened his eyes and said he had no idea what she was talking about.

One evening, about a month after Colin Clarke's arrival, Ba didn't come home for dinner. The following evening, it happened again. Hours later, when he finally returned, Ma hurried down the stairs. The door to the study swung shut and the arguing started. I lay awake in bed, listening; I was old enough to know something was seriously wrong.

At first my parents' voices were too soft for me to hear, but then I heard the American's name, spoken by Ba in that hideous accent, and my mother's voice rose in a shriek. Images from that night came back to me: the way Ma had laughed wildly at Colin Clarke's jokes, how at the end of the night, his wife had refrained from taking Ma's hand, instead raising her palm in a half-hearted wave. My parents' voices grew steadily louder, and when I could listen no longer, I got out of bed and ran the faucet in the tub at full blast. There in the warm bath I lay, watching my fingers and toes shrivel as if from old age.

My parents' argument stretched through the week. On day four,

Ba peeked into my room after midnight, walked through the half-open door of the en suite bathroom and found me asleep in a tub of tepid water. He wrapped me in a large, fluffy towel and carried me to bed.

The next morning, the two of us drove to Uncle Robert and Auntie Tina's house, where I was to stay while he and Ma took care of "grown-up business." I didn't point out I was too old to be spoken to like that.

The drive over was the first time we'd been alone together in days, and I was both furious at him and comforted by his presence. Unable to put my conflicting emotions into words, I simply asked, "When can I come home?"

"Soon," my father said. "In a few days, your ma or I will come get you."

Divorce was still rare in Singapore — I'd learned of its occurrence from books, the way I'd once learned of Santa Claus — but I worried all the same. What would it take to drive my mother back to her beloved America?

In front of my uncle's house, Ba stretched his lips into a tired smile, and I tried to smile back. As much as I longed to ask questions, I sensed this wasn't the time, and that he might not even have the answers.

In hindsight, it's difficult to isolate how much or how little I knew about my parents' conflict. At any rate, not long after my four-day stay at Uncle Robert's, my dear friend Kat intervened.

Kat is three months younger than me but has always seemed older, especially when we were kids. Thanks to the influence of her big sister, Kat was the first to start using eye shadow and the first to have a co-ed birthday party. She was also the first to educate me on the distinctly Singaporean, postcolonial phenomenon of "sarong party girls" or "SPGs."

That afternoon, Kat, our other best friend Cindy, and I were on our stomachs on Kat's bed, watching the movie, *Pretty Woman*. This was the early nineties, and R-rated movies were censored before being permitted in the country. Nonetheless, Kat's mum made us fast-forward through the beginning, which she deemed unsuitable for girls our age. Despite the missing scenes, I took in the way the posh shop girls glared down their long, thin noses, and understood there was something shameful about the lead actress, without fully grasping that she was a prostitute.

We three watched in silence, captivated by the palm-tree-lined boulevards, the fancy cars, the swirling dresses and matching hats—none of which were anything like the America my mother had described. When the final scene faded to black, Kat rolled onto one side and propped herself up on an elbow. "You know," she said casually, "there are women like that in Singapore."

Something in her tone signaled danger. I proceeded with caution. "What do you mean?"

"Singaporean ladies who only date *ang mos*," she said, using the Chinese slang word for "Caucasian." She explained that her parents had taken the family to the beach at Sentosa, where her sister had pointed out the SPGs—local women in animal-print bikinis and short shorts, with fake *ang mo* highlights and fake *ang mo* accents, who flirted with all the rich, *ang mo* men.

A pejorative term roughly antonymous to a man with an Asian fetish, an SPG is by no means a sex worker. But given that we were ten-year-olds sheltered by both government and parental censorship, Kat's murky equating of prostitutes and SPGs was understandable.

Unsure of where this conversation was heading, I glanced at Cindy to see if she had as many questions as I did, but she lowered her eyes, mesmerized by the tassels hanging off the bedspread. I suspected she'd heard this all before.

Kat watched me carefully as she spoke. "My sister asked me if your mum was a sarong party girl, but of course I said no, *lah*! Those ladies dress like sluts. And they're young."

This only confused me further. Again I looked for Cindy to affirm the ridiculousness of Kat's assertion. She avoided my gaze and scrunched up her face like she'd eaten a Super Lemon hard candy. I thought back to my parents' battle: something had happened between Ma and the American, something too grotesque to unravel.

I wondered who else knew. Earlier that day, when Kat's mum had picked us up from school, she had asked after my parents. I hadn't thought much of it then, but now I wondered if she hadn't perhaps seemed extra concerned, like she wasn't just asking to be polite. How would she have found out about Ma and Ba's battle? And what of my friends at school? Who else had Kat told?

Forcing back tears, I asked to use the phone in the other room. My mother answered, and in a choked voice, I begged her to pick me up right away.

Fifteen minutes later, she pulled up at the gate, waving breezily from the driver's seat.

Even now, I can still recall the smirk on Kat's face—the narrowed eyes and half smile that belonged to someone twice her age.

• • •

Later, after I'd left for boarding school and stopped thinking of my parents' house as home, I summoned the courage to question my mother, and of course, she told the truth.

In the years since, I've replayed her words, filling in blanks, adding detail—so much so that the scenes unspool in my mind like a film reel, like something I've witnessed with my own eyes.

The day after the disastrous welcome dinner, the vivacious lecturer finds herself at the door of the distinguished visitor's office. There, she hesitates, quaking, already struggling with the pretense that she has come to apologize. But then she takes a deep breath and raps firmly on the door. He tells her to come in. He is tall and imposing, trim for a man of his age. He invites her to take a seat and brushes off her apology with a hearty American laugh. They continue their discussion from the night before; then, he inquires about her research on Dualla Misipo, or maybe Kum'a Ndumbe III, both Cameroonian writers who wrote in German.

Before long, half an hour has passed, and then another, and then one of them suggests they leave campus to carry on their conversation over a drink. One, or maybe both, glances at a wristwatch; neither points out that it is only three o'clock.

The boozy afternoon stretches late into evening—and then into other evenings spent at corner tables in quiet, dimly lit restaurants, or at the symphony, or in one of their offices, the door ajar, talking about books.

Try as I may, I can't recall seeing my mother drunk back then. Maybe she was careful to sober up first. Maybe I didn't know what to look for. Or maybe she only came home after my father had tucked me into bed.

It seems irrelevant—the fact that no matter how late she stayed out, she always came home. Or that although the American told her she was too brilliant to remain at this second-rate institution, although he begged her to come to Chicago, promised to find her work, and vowed to leave his pouffy-haired wife, theirs was a purely platonic affair. Here, on our tiny, insular island, that Ma and the American were seen together at all was scandal enough.

My mother had distanced herself from her own parents ever since they'd pressured her to return home, so I can only imagine their distress. Ahkong and Amah, on the other hand, made their outrage known. They'd never approved of my parents' marriage in the first place, and now they planted themselves at our dining table and urged their son to cut his losses and start over, as I listened, stricken, from upstairs. This was the moment when I first understood that my parents and I made up a single, precarious unit. Everyone else, no matter how well-intentioned, would always be a potential threat.

Thankfully, once again, Ba defied his parents. My father and mother remained together, and in time, from my perspective at least, life returned to normal.

In the months following their reconciliation, Ba rarely missed dinner at home. Ma instructed the maid to prepare *boeuf bourguignon* and pork tenderloin with apples and rack of lamb—all the foods Ba loved that Ma thought were too heavy for every day. When my parents walked down the street, they held hands, their fingers loosely interlocked. For Ma's fortieth birthday, they flew to San Sebastian and returned with sunglass tans and handwritten menus from Michelin-starred restaurants. Ma even stopped reminiscing about her years in America. Over a decade into their marriage, she finally seemed ready to embrace her life in Singapore.

As much as it thrilled me to see my parents happy, I came to understand that even within our little family of three, the two of them were a single unit all to themselves. How else to explain why, when Ma started drinking more, opening a bottle of wine at dinner, sipping glass after glass late into the night, Ba devoted his energy to hiding her behavior from me?

And yet, since my return, there were times when it was easy to overlook the stress that Ma's illness and drinking had placed on their marriage. Over the past weeks, I'd walked in on my parents sitting on the loveseat in front of the television with their forearms intertwined—a position that seemed almost unconscious. Times like these, I wanted to believe that no matter how deep Ma's betrayal, Ba had found a way to forgive; that despite all Ma had given up, she had arrived at contentment.

8

Now that the situation with Cal had been resolved, and Uncle Robert had assured my father that he had everything under control, Ba was easing back into retirement. He aimed to spend no more than two days a week at Lin's, and so, on Monday, I drove to work without him.

I'd taken one day off to accompany my parents to the hospital, but when I arrived at the office, it felt like I'd been gone for weeks. Although it was barely eight thirty, the whole floor bustled with activity. The sales and marketing people were holed up in the conference room with binders as thick as unabridged dictionaries. The two finance guys hurried back and forth between their cubes. Even Shuting was too busy to look up when I walked past.

I dropped my purse on my desk and went straight to Frankie's office, where I found her with Jason from sales.

"Thanks for getting me these numbers on such short notice," she said with a dazzling smile.

Jason slid his hands in his pockets and raised his shoulders to his ears. "Any time you need something, just let me know." He nodded at me as he walked out, pausing to grab a fistful of pens off the shelf that still held the office's spare supplies.

"What time did everyone get here?" I asked.

Frankie looked tanned and even blonder from her trip to the beach with my friends. When she turned her head, the tip of her ear was pink with sunburn. "Haven't you heard? The Mama Poon people are coming to visit."

I was familiar with Mama Poon's, the trendy California-based grocery store chain that experts proclaimed was revolutionizing the food retail sector. One had opened up down the street from my San Francisco apartment right before I moved back to Singapore. I'd spent an hour wandering the aisles, filling my cart with Japanese crackers wrapped in cherry blossom–patterned rice paper and red foil tubes of chocolate-covered marzipan, in addition to my regular staples. Like all the other branches, the store was set up to resemble a seaside shack, complete with upbeat staff clad in bright Hawaiian shirts.

I tried to imagine those same workers traipsing through our office. "What are they doing here?"

Frankie gestured for me to take a seat. She explained that the grocery store chain was expanding their private-label line — products sourced from factories all over the world to be sold under the Mama Poon name. One of those products was to be soy sauce, and Mama Poon's legendary founder, Benji Rosenthal himself, had narrowed down the contending factories to one in Kuala Lumpur, one in Tainan, and us.

"He'll be here tomorrow. To sample our fiberglass sauce," Frankie said.

When I looked unimpressed, she tried again. "Benji Rosenthal is coming to Lin's. *The* Benji Rosenthal."

Benji Rosenthal was an aging hippie with a waist-length, graying ponytail, whose path to capitalistic success had been mythologized in business school case studies across America. He'd spent the eighties surfing and sampling weed all over Southeast Asia. Along the way, he befriended Mama Pun, an elderly Thai woman. In exchange for manual labor and household chores, Mama Pun gave him the spare bedroom that had belonged to her recently deceased son. When her arthritis all but paralyzed her, Benji Rosenthal took over the cooking for their household of two. Under her strict supervision, he learned to prepare coconut milk–based curries, spicy, tangy salads and the hearty meat- or oyster-filled omelets that are the staples of central Thai cuisine. He went on to care for the old woman until the day she died.

When he returned to California, Benji Rosenthal discovered how difficult it was to recreate his favorite dishes without cardamom, Thai coriander, galangal root. Nostalgia coupled with frustration drove him to open a small market in Santa Barbara, named Mama Poon's in honor of his old friend, whose name he anglicized for branding purposes. In the years since, that single market had become a chain of full-fledged grocery stores offering exotic produce at superior value. Eighteen locations had sprung up across California, Oregon, and Washington; three more would open on the East Coast in the coming year.

"I get it," I said. "This visit is a big deal. But we just started experimenting with fiberglass tanks. We don't know if this new sauce is going to be any good." After the debacle with Cal's ready-to-cook sauces, I would have expected my uncle to proceed with caution. I myself had never tasted the new product, but Ba had assured me it would be *gao sai* — a description that struck me as more humorous and less disgusting than if it'd been spoken in English: dog shit.

Frankie shrugged. "That's for Benji Rosenthal to decide. What do you expect us to do? Turn him away?"

"Point taken," I said.

She nodded firmly and scratched the sunburned tip of her ear.

"How was the beach?"

"It was fantastic," she said.

"I had a good weekend, too." I waited for Frankie to ask about my mother and to tell me I'd been missed.

"Oh, good. I'm glad," she said, and went on to outline all the tasks we needed to tackle that day.

I didn't have to wait long to taste Lin's new fiberglass sauce. I was sitting at my desk, staring at my cell phone and willing James to call, when Uncle Robert summoned Frankie and me to his office.

My uncle was standing by the window with his back to us, holding a small bottle to the light. When he heard us enter, he turned. "Welcome to the future," he said. "Lin's soy sauce 2.0." Mr. Liu, Lin's head scientist, had sent up a prototype of the sauce we would present to the team from Mama Poon's.

I took the bottle from my uncle's extended hand. It was still warm from his palm. Holding the bottle at eye level, I saw that the sauce was dark and murky, almost opaque — so different from the tawny translucence of our clay-aged brew.

"Now, Gretchen, you know it's not going to taste like our premium sauce," Uncle Robert warned as he slid a white porcelain dish across his desk. He turned to Frankie. "She has a palate like her father's."

"Lucky for you, I'm out of practice," I said. I poured out the sauce and took a few short sniffs, searching for the citrus top notes and round caramel base that distinguished our trademark brew.

But this sauce smelled thick and meaty, as flat and dull as an old coin. I dipped the tip of my pinkie finger in the sauce and dabbed it on my tongue. A burst of salty-sweet assaulted my palate, and then vanished almost instantly, leaving a watery, metallic aftertaste.

Suddenly I was relieved the sauce hadn't exceeded my expectations. "Is this the best Mr. Liu can do?" I asked.

My uncle sighed. He dipped his pinkie finger in the dish of sauce, then placed the finger in his mouth and sucked audibly. He closed his eyes for an instant and said, "It's not ideal."

"You can say that again," I said with a laugh. I had yet to grasp the gravity of the situation, how a partnership with Mama Poon's could shape the company for years to come.

Ignoring my comment, my uncle pushed the dish across the table to Frankie. She stuck her finger in the dish, just as my uncle and I had, and tasted the sauce. For someone who had only been through one soy sauce tasting, she certainly projected confidence.

Uncle Robert said, "Keep in mind-ah, this sauce is cheaper and has a longer shelf life than our premium sauce. Exactly what Mama Poon's is looking for."

Frankie ran her tongue over her front teeth and said, "Honestly, it tastes pretty good to me."

My head snapped toward her, and she added, "I mean, given the circumstances."

"Precisely," my uncle said. "We must be realistic."

"Robert's right," she said, looking straight at me as though I'd disagreed. She didn't seem to notice that everyone else called my uncle "Mr. Lin." She went on, "This fiberglass sauce is for a different consumer base. Will Mama Poon's customers really be able to tell the difference?"

I stopped myself from pointing out that naysayers had told Ah-kong exactly the same thing over fifty years earlier. Uncle Robert had asked me to try the sauce, and I'd told him what I thought. All this other stuff — the fiberglass tanks, the Mama Poon deal, the US Expansion Project — was their concern. They didn't need to justify anything to me.

But even as I fought to establish how little I cared, I couldn't help but wonder what my grandfather would have thought of Mama Poon's. Especially since just last week Frankie and I had concluded that Lin's needed to embrace its traditional brewing methods, expanding the reach of its premium sauces as opposed to pursuing commercial ventures.

"Has my father tasted this?" I asked.

My uncle planted his elbows on his desk and rested his chin in his palms. His fingers cupped his full cheeks, and for an instant I caught a glimpse of the boy he must have been, Ah Xiong's younger brother. "Let's just say, he'd rather not get involved," he said. He sat up in his chair and stretched out his arms like an opera singer about to burst into an aria. "But that's the thing about business, *lah*. You can't pick a path and blindly follow it."

"I agree," said Frankie. "Success is all about being nimble. Adapting to change."

The two of them exchanged satisfied smiles, and I resolved to keep my mouth shut for the rest of the meeting.

Down below in the courtyard, beyond my uncle's window, a worker in a wide-brimmed straw hat made his way up and down the rows of clay jars, a long wooden paddle in hand. At each jar, he lifted the lid, inserted the paddle and gave the mixture a few good stirs.

As a child, I'd loved to traipse behind the worker on duty in my matching knee-length polo shirt, standing on my tiptoes to peek over the lip of each jar, offering advice and begging to help. If I begged hard enough, and the worker wasn't too pressed for time, he let me wrap my fists around the paddle, and I gritted my teeth, squinted through the sweat and stirred as best I could. Even from up here, in Uncle Robert's air-conditioned office, I could still conjure up the tart, briny smell of the fermenting beans; I could feel the jar's contents shift around my paddle like a living thing.

My uncle explained that Frankie and I would need to spend the rest of the afternoon putting together slides for the next day's presentation. "We don't have much time, so I appreciate your flexibility."

In the courtyard, down below, the worker finished stirring the last jar. He mopped the sweat from his forehead with the sleeve of his yellow polo shirt and hung the paddle from a hook on the wall.

By six in the evening, Frankie and I were still hours away from completing our task. I didn't mind having to stay late; it wasn't as if I had anywhere else to be.

On his way out, my uncle knocked on my door. He had a Styrofoam food container in one hand. "I told Mr. Liu to keep working on the sauce," he said. "Of course there's always room for improvement, *lah*. Sometimes we forget." His words were jolly, but he looked haggard. His skin was gray and dull; his cheeks sagged with their own weight. For the first time I thought about how challenging it must be for him to take over this project from his son.

I said, "I'm sorry if I was being difficult. From now on I'll leave the strategizing to you and Frankie."

He gave me a sad smile. "You're doing a great job. I know your father is proud of you."

I wondered how it felt to lose faith in one's own child. Did Uncle Robert blame himself for Cal's mistakes?

For as long as I could remember, my cousin had been fearless. He had a way of intimidating everyone around him, even his own mother. In elementary school, I'd often played board games with Lily and Rose at their house. Cal never joined us. He was four years older and by then a moody teenager. But once when our round of Monopoly got a little out of hand, and our shrieking grew too loud, he stormed out of his dark cave of a room and swept his arm across the board. Tiny red and blue and green houses rained into my lap. I was too frightened to speak. If my uncle had been home, he would have reprimanded Cal, who would receive the scolding with his head lowered but his eyes hard as stone. Even when being told off, my cousin showed no fear.

"Uncle Robert," I said, "how is Cal handling the news?"

My uncle recoiled. "He's fine," he said, too loudly. He looked down and seemed startled to find the Styrofoam container in his hands. He set the container on my desk. "Left over from lunch," he said, not meeting my eyes. "Don't stay too late, yah? Frankie too." And then he was gone.

Soon Frankie and I were the only ones left in the building.

When we were too famished to keep working, she and I convened in the break room. Sitting on the counter by the sink, we passed my uncle's leftovers back and forth, first attempting to eat the cold noodles with plastic knives we found in a mug on a shelf, then giving up and using our fingers.

Without giving away that Cal had been fired, I tried to explain to Frankie why my exchange with my uncle had so affected me. "I feel sorry for him," I said. "He may be the president of the company, but he can't make a decision without everyone else getting involved." I smiled, remembering my mother's reaction to the office's new pale-pistachio walls: she'd threatened to bring in her own team of painters in the middle of the night.

"He watched your father go through the same thing," Frankie said. "He certainly knew what he was getting into."

Her lack of sympathy surprised me. "Maybe so, but it's still a tough situation to be in. And that's not to say that I approve of this new sauce. No one would have dared mention the word 'fiberglass' in front of my grandfather."

Frankie wiped off her fingers with a paper towel, patted the concave space where her belly used to be and said she was done eating. Even though I was still hungry, I felt compelled to stop, too.

She said, "From everything I've heard, your grandfather was a risk taker. You never know. He might have backed this particular risk."

All day long she'd disagreed with everything I'd said, and now, eleven hours into the workday, I was annoyed. I said. "Lin's makes soy sauce. Mouthwatering, handmade soy sauce. That fiberglass crap isn't up to standard."

She held up her hands in surrender, which only annoyed me further. She said, "Okay, you're right, what do I know?" She filled a glass with water from the faucet, drained it and refilled it. "Want some?" she asked, holding out the glass to me.

I shook my head. In an effort to smooth things over, I said, "Tell me about your weekend."

Her face lit up. "You'll never believe what your crazy friend Kat talked me into doing."

"What?" I asked amiably.

"I bought a bikini. My very first."

"You went shopping with Kat?" I tried to keep my tone neutral.

"Yeah, on Friday, after work," she said, and went on to tell me about the trip to the beach, and about the impromptu beach volleyball tournament they'd gotten roped into. "Co-ed teams," she said. "Thankfully, Pierre and James showed up."

My entire body froze. "James?"

"Yeah, he came with Pierre," she said, then stopped when she saw my face. "Oh, I thought you knew."

I said nothing.

"But you already had plans," she said. "To stay home with your mom."

"I did."

"How's she doing?"

"Much better, thank you for asking," I said.

Frankie leaned in close. "And what's going on with you and James?"

I wanted to share everything, truly I did. Would Frankie think I'd committed a fatal error by going home with James on the first date? I loathed myself for letting that thought cross my mind, and then I loathed myself for obsessing about this man who was so clearly not interested in me. Determined not to waste another second on him, I said, "It was only one date. I don't even think I'm going to see him again."

She didn't back down. "Are you sure you're all right?"

I glanced at the clock on the microwave. Eight-thirty. "We should get back to work."

She studied me for another beat or two, then yawned and stretched out her arms. "How much longer can they expect us to go on without Cal?" she asked.

It was a rhetorical question, but I seized the opportunity to shift the balance of power back in my favor. Uncle Robert would make his announcement soon, and I saw no harm in telling her the truth. "Frankie," I said, "Cal's gone." I went on to repeat what my father had told me, the stunned expression on her face a minor consolation.

At nine o'clock, we agreed to come in early the next morning, and then I gave her a ride home.

Back in my parents' house, someone, probably Cora, had left an official-looking envelope on my desk. The return address was in San Francisco, and immediately I knew the letter had come from a lawyer writing on behalf of Paul. A familiar panic rushed through me: the feeling that no matter how much air I gulped down, suffocation was imminent.

Somehow I steadied my hands and tore open the envelope, only to find myself staring at a letter from the conservatory, requesting a deposit to hold my place for the upcoming semester.

I closed my eyes. My breathing slowed. And then I was standing on the corner of Franklin and Oak, the strains of a lone trumpet drifting from the window of a practice room, the breeze swirling a pile of yellow leaves about my feet, the sunlight so bright I could barely open my eyes.

I signed the form without reading it, found a stamp for the envelope, and placed it in the very center of my desk, as though without the reminder I would forget to ask my father for a check.

9

FRANKIE AND I HAD JUST COMPLETED the final edits on the slides for my uncle's presentation when the door to the conference room swung open. Someone hit the light switch and the recessed bulbs blinked on one at a time.

My uncle came in first. He'd dressed up for the occasion in a long-sleeved button-up shirt, instead of the threadbare short-sleeved shirts he favored. I gave him an encouraging smile, but he didn't seem to notice.

Entering close behind him was the legendary Benji Rosenthal: middle-aged, tall, narrow and sinewy as a modern dancer, and clad in his trademark Hawaiian shirt. He apparently dressed up for no one. He was accompanied by his assistant, a lanky boy in a matching shirt who looked barely old enough to have graduated college.

After everyone had been introduced, we took our seats around the table—us in our freshly pressed business casual, them in their beachwear—and Frankie dimmed the lights.

But instead of signaling me to cue up the slides, Uncle Robert pushed back his shirt cuff and squinted at his watch. A frown settled on his face and he shifted in his chair. I'd never seen him so edgy. Now he squared his shoulders, sat back and asked Benji Rosenthal about his flight, and whether he would have a chance to do a bit of sightseeing while he was here.

Frankie and I shot each other looks.

"Unfortunately we have to head straight to the airport after this meeting," said Benji Rosenthal. He had a booming, resonant voice and twinkling eyes that made him look like he was about to tell a joke.

Apparently uninterested in the conversation, the assistant studied the mobile device in his palm.

"Yes, of course," said Uncle Robert. "But what a pity to come all this way and not have time to see anything." He gave his watch another peek and began to list the various tourist attractions the Americans would miss: Jurong Bird Park, the night safari at the Mandai Zoo, Chinatown, of course, where preparations for the upcoming Hungry Ghost Festival were well underway.

Across the table, Frankie tilted her head toward the light switch on the back wall, questioning if she should turn the lights back on, or if we should all continue chatting in the dim glow of the overhead projector. I shook my head almost imperceptibly.

That's when the door swung open.

"Sure, definitely," someone was saying to an unknown listener. "Catch up later, yah?"

I immediately recognized the voice.

A polished brown loafer stepped through the doorway, followed by a gray pant leg, a pink shirtsleeve. "I'm so sorry I'm late," said

Cal. His expansive smile assured us he had a perfectly good explanation for his delay—so perfect that there was no need to actually explain.

Frankie's mouth hung open. When I met her gaze, she sealed her lips and looked away. I couldn't tell if she was upset with me, or simply flabbergasted. I wanted to clarify that I hadn't lied to her, that I was as taken aback as she was.

Uncle Robert was shaking his head in disapproval but could not mask his pleasure. "Meet my son," he said to Benji Rosenthal. "My oldest. Do you have children?"

"Not that I know of," the American said with a wink, then, more soberly, "Just my company."

Only the assistant gave a short bark of a laugh.

"Calvin Lin," Cal said, extending a hand to Benji Rosenthal. "A pleasure and an honor to meet you." My cousin's large, even teeth gleamed bright white against his broad face. His skin was deeply bronzed from the time he'd spent in the Maldives, waiting for news of his future at Lin's. He introduced himself to the assistant and then to Frankie, patting the back of her hand and telling her he'd heard only good things. She blushed and ducked her head.

When he came around to my side of the table, he thumped me between my shoulder blades, hard, and said, "Welcome back, Gretch."

"Same to you," I said, looking straight at my uncle.

Uncle Robert's gaze flickered over to the projector screen and up at the ceiling and down at his hands, but never landed on me. "Let's get started, shall we?" he said.

Index finger poised over my laptop keyboard, I imagined pushing back my chair, leaping up and sprinting down the hallway to call Ba.

At breakfast that morning, my father had been invisible behind his newspaper as I shoveled cereal in my mouth and tried to gulp down coffee without scalding my tongue. I was running to the door with a half-eaten piece of toast when it occurred to me to ask if he planned to stop by the office. "Don't you want to at least shake hands with the famous Benji Rosenthal?"

Ba lowered the paper so we were face to face. A fold of puffy skin sagged beneath each eye. He'd had trouble sleeping ever since our meeting with Ma's doctor. He said, "Your uncle doesn't need my help. He's made that clear."

In my haste to get to work, I didn't register that Uncle Robert had claimed the opposite, that Ba was the one who wanted nothing to do with the Mama Poon deal.

There was no way my father knew Cal was back.

Uncle Robert cleared his throat. This time he glared right at me.

I jabbed the return key. The cheerful red script of the first slide, "How We Got Here," filled the screen.

My uncle launched into the history of Lin's Soy Sauce, and I turned my attention to Cal. How dare he saunter in like this, as if he had nothing to apologize for, as if he hadn't failed his father, my father, the entire family.

I pulled up the next slide. Uncle Robert, now fully in his element, veered from his notes to deliver an anecdote about Ahkong's failed early attempts to sell his beloved sauce. In the beginning, he explained, shopkeepers were skittish about taking on a new product, especially one that was priced so much higher than the brands they already stocked. Determined to demonstrate that his sauce was worth the extra money, Ahkong refused to offer a discount. In his first week, he visited over twenty provision shops across the island, and each time he was turned away. Driven by desperation, he hit on the idea of lugging a very heavy clay jar on a dolly from store to store to illustrate his special fermentation process. Perhaps out of pity, the first shopkeeper he dropped in on with his jar agreed to a taste, which led to Ahkong's very first sale.

Benji Rosenthal asked, "How much does one of those things weigh anyway?"

"Almost twenty-five kilograms," Uncle Robert said. "You see, he truly was desperate."

Benji Rosenthal slapped the table and fairly guffawed, and my uncle beamed.

I cringed, thinking about how my grandfather would have reacted to this scene: stories about his hard work being used to peddle Lin's first fiberglass-aged sauce. How Ahkong would have dealt with Cal's misdeeds, I couldn't say for sure, but I did know my uncle would never have dared go behind his own father's back to reinstate his son.

Even though I'd been around for barely a month, Uncle Robert's betrayal felt as personal as Paul's lies about Sue.

Seventeen years earlier, during my first stint at Lin's, I'd spent the school holidays alongside Cal who was back on the bottling line for the third year in a row. My cousin didn't bother to warn me about the grueling nature of the work. Even with the ceiling fans whirring at full-blast, the factory floor was suffocatingly hot. Three hours into my first eight-hour shift, my quads began to ache—an ache that wouldn't entirely subside until two days after I'd left the factory. But while I tried to elicit sympathy for my sore legs and sweat-soaked clothes, Cal worked diligently, never complaining, breaking his silence only to tell me, with a Zen Buddhist's calm, that fixating on my discomfort would make things worse.

After those early days at the factory, I gave up trying to connect with Cal. Instead I got to know other workers on the line — middle-aged women who were kind and friendly and never made me sweep the floors. They told me about the old days at Lin's, and about their children, some of whom were around my age. At half past noon, when we all gathered for lunch, the workers patted me on the head and told my grandfather I was doing a fine job.

One particularly humid day near the end of my month-long tenure, when Cal and I and the other workers filed in the dining room, Ahkong beckoned for me to sit between him and Ba. He filled my bowl with clear winter melon soup and tipped in some soy sauce. "*Jiak,*" he urged.

The soup was hot and I blew on my soupspoon before sipping with care. "Weird," was the word that left my mouth. I kept eating.

"Weird how?" Ba set down his own spoon.

Ahkong leaned in.

I wasn't sure why they were behaving so strangely. "Just weird," I said in between bites. My grandfather had poured less than a teaspoon of soy sauce in my bowl, but that small amount had made the soup too salty. I pointed to the plastic dispenser. "That isn't our sauce."

Ahkong threw back his head and laughed. The rest of the table applauded, and I felt pleased but also sheepish. After all, it was Ba who had taught me, years earlier, to isolate and identify the different layers of flavor in our own light sauce.

Ahkong pulled out a bright red ten-dollar bill and handed it to me. He turned to Ba and said in Chinese, "This little gourd is going to be a success."

"She got lucky," Ba said, though his smile was full and warm.

Later, Cal and I left the dining room together, and as the glass door swung shut behind us, he took my wrist and pulled me aside. Not caring that there were other workers around, he leaned in so close I could smell the ginger on his breath. I backed up flat against the wall.

"Stop sucking up to everyone, you hear me?" he said.

I nodded automatically.

"You're just a kid. You don't know anything."

Again I nodded.

"Good. Let's go." He turned and marched across the courtyard, and I hurried behind him, glad the month was almost over.

The following year, when I was fourteen, I begged to be exempted from factory work like my girl cousins — Lily because she had severe asthma, and Rose because she spent her holidays at ballet camp. Unlike them, I had no good excuse, but Ba relented after I formed an alliance with my mother by agreeing to double my practice time at the piano. Eventually, my father accepted my lack of interest in soy sauce, and turned his attention to Cal.

Now my uncle was listing the many accolades our sauce had earned: Tasty Singapore Brand Ambassador, Asia Star Award, Golden Excellency Award, Singapore Heritage Award. Benji Rosenthal tented his fingertips and closed his eyes. He was either listening intently or not listening at all. My uncle kept going.

I wondered where he'd been, those seventeen years earlier, on the afternoon of my grandfather's test. I didn't recall Uncle Robert sitting at the table, but I could picture him somewhere in the dining room, watching me in silence, plotting even then for his own son to get ahead. How could I reconcile this image of Uncle Robert with the man I knew? Of all my relatives, he was the one I felt closest to, the one I trusted most.

The conference room lights blinked back on, and Benji Rosenthal opened his eyes. The assistant put aside his mobile device for the first time. My uncle grinned at the Americans, and Cal rolled his head in a languid circle, as if he'd just awaken from a nap.

"Well, listen," Benji Rosenthal said, gazing around the room to include each and every one of us. "This is impressive. Really impressive."

"Wait until you try our sauce," Cal said, reaching for the tray I'd arranged on the table.

With practiced ease, he served the sauce to the Americans. I sat back and watched as he instructed them to lean in and inhale its bouquet. "Like you're sniffing a glass of your favorite wine."

Just as no one had pointed out that Lin's awards and accolades had been earned by our premium sauces, no one pointed out that the predominant flavor of this new sauce was a harsh metallic tang.

We watched as Benji Rosenthal dipped his rice cracker in the dish and tossed it in his mouth. At that moment, I wanted nothing more than for him to scrunch up his face, pull back and holler that it was like sucking on a rusty nail.

"Great," the American said before he finished chewing. "Perfect. This is exactly what we want for our stores."

"Great. Just great," his assistant chimed in.

My uncle's jaw softened. He'd been right all along. Benji Rosenthal couldn't tell the difference, and neither would the shoppers at Mama Poon's. The sauce was good enough.

Around the table, everyone stood, and I did too. Benji Rosenthal promised to be in touch once he'd completed his last factory visit. His eyes twinkled as he said to Uncle Robert, "But between you and me, my mind's already made up."

We all shook hands and told each other how nice it was to have finally met.

"Excellent work," Uncle Robert said to Frankie. "Excellent work," he repeated to me.

I gave him a cold, probing regard, but he absently patted my shoulder and gazed past my ear.

Cal and Uncle Robert escorted the Americans down the hallway, neither indicating that Frankie and I should come along. As the men disappeared down the stairs, Benji Rosenthal's voice boomed above the others. "You know," he said, "Mama Poon's really is a family business. So it's swell to have found another company so aligned with our values and ideals."

Cal's response: "I grew up right here in this factory, and I wouldn't have had it any other way. It truly is home."

Inside the conference room, Frankie shut her laptop and collapsed back in her chair. I dropped my head in my hands, suddenly overcome by fatigue.

After a while, Frankie asked, "What do we do now?"

And then we heard voices hurtling back up the stairs — Uncle Robert's and Cal's and a third that belonged to Ba.

I rushed to the door, Frankie close behind. Peering out of the conference room, we found all our co-workers similarly positioned.

"No," we heard my father say, his voice ricocheting from the stairwell. "You and I are going to settle this now."

I checked the time. He must have left Ma at the hospital and hurried over. Who had called to tell him about Cal? Perhaps it was Mr. Liu. A Lin's employee for over fifty years, he surely had strong feelings about how the company was run. Perhaps Shuting had called, for once channeling her drama-vulture energy into something worthwhile. Perhaps Ba had figured it out himself as he sat with Ma in the dialysis room, going over previous conversations with my uncle, half-watching Melody on TV.

The trio emerged from the stairwell. Uncle Robert's forehead was creased with worry. Cal was sweating through the armpits of his pink shirt. Only Ba's face was still as a mask.

On the office floor, heads darted back into cubes, but I didn't move. I didn't care if they caught me watching; I wanted to be seen.

"Please, *Kor*," my uncle murmured to Ba. *Elder brother.*

"We can explain everything," said Cal.

Ba stopped short. He looked straight at my cousin. "You will explain nothing." He turned to Uncle Robert. "I'm sorry, but he cannot be here." Ba swept past Cal, who staggered back against the wall. He turned the knob to my uncle's office, but before he stepped in something made him pause. He looked up and, for the first time, noticed me.

"Ba." My lips formed the word, but no sound came out.

My father's face relaxed. He seemed to exhale. And then he and my uncle entered the office, shutting the door behind them, lowering the blinds.

Inside that impenetrable room, voices rose and fell. Something landed on the floor with a weighty thud. Cal kept standing there staring at the door, feet rooted to the same exact spot, neck muscles straining from his shirt collar, hands clenched into fists.

It took me a second to notice the tension in my own neck and shoulders, the way my fingers curled inwards, stabbing my nails into my palms. I thought of the deposit resting on my desk, waiting to be mailed to the conservatory. I felt lucky to have some place else to go.

10

WHEN MY MOTHER FIRST PROPOSED boarding school in Monterey, California, my father swiftly shot down the idea, which only piqued my interest. I pictured boys in hip-slung board shorts, with sandy hair and rippling abs. In reality, my future classmates were precocious and studious and obsessed with getting into top-tier universities — one of the reasons Ba eventually changed his mind.

I'd been away at school for no more than two weeks when Ba sent my first care package: an entire case of sample-size bottles of Lin's light soy sauce, which I hid under the bed. Times when I couldn't eat another bite of cafeteria meatloaf, or chili, or casserole, I retreated to my room with a bowl of rice pilaf, or, when the situation was desperate, pasta, and broke into my stash.

My mother sent lovely impractical things like letterpress birthday cards, or a pair of angora mittens I rarely needed through the mild

Monterey winters. Once, around Thanksgiving, she sent a box of twelve perfectly ripe Comice pears.

On Sundays, after I waited in line at one of two dorm pay phones, my parents and I talked for ten or fifteen minutes, never more. After all there were other students who needed the phone. I told my parents about the weather, my classes, my latest cross-country meet or piano recital. They passed on messages from my grandparents and updates on my cousins. Sometimes they ended with "love you," other times they forgot.

By the end of my first semester, I'd shed my homesickness like a snake its skin. Throughout Christmas break in Singapore, I counted the days until my return to school, and my parents were proud of how well I'd adjusted.

Only once did I catch a glimpse of my mother's ambivalence. At the end of that first Christmas break, I awoke at five in the morning to make my flight. The entire drive to the airport I dozed in the backseat until an abrupt swerve of the car roused me. Eyes still closed, I heard a quiet sobbing noise so unfamiliar I wasn't immediately sure what it was. Opening one eye, I saw my mother's head pressed against the windowpane. With one hand on the steering wheel, my father reached his other hand to her. "All right?" he asked softly. "Of course," she sobbed. I shut my eyes and pretended to be asleep. It was the one time I'd see her cry.

Even now, with all she'd gone through, Ma continued to impress me with her strength and stoicism. She hadn't had a drink in almost a week. She'd stood back and let me get rid of every bottle in the house. She was practicing the piano daily, though she continued to boycott my metronome, going so far as to return the wooden pyramid to its perch on my nightstand.

Especially in the beginning, Ma's doctor had informed us, most people actually found it easier to give up alcohol altogether. "'No' can be much less complicated than 'maybe,'" Dr. Yeoh said with a meaningful look. I tried to discern the deeper message behind his words.

I was thinking about "no's" and "maybe's" and the paradox of too much choice when I walked through the front door, hours after Cal's surprise appearance.

Ma was practicing her Debussy piece. She lifted her fingers off the keys. "Auntie Tina called," she said, her gaze pointing to my father in the dining room.

He and I had left work in separate cars, and now he sat at the table cracking his knuckles and muttering to himself.

Ma told me that my aunt, Uncle Robert's wife, had invited everyone to a family dinner that evening. She glanced over at Ba one last time, put aside her sheet music, and went to get dressed.

As if the family were gathering to celebrate some joyous occasion, my aunt had reserved a private room at Imperial Treasure, the city's best Shanghainese restaurant, and a longtime Lin's client—hence their willingness to accommodate all eleven of us on such short notice. The restaurant was located on Orchard Road, on the top floor of a massive high-end shopping center surrounded by glossy office towers.

Having neglected to take the elevator, my father, my mother, and I found ourselves on one escalator after another, from the third-basement car park up through seven brightly lit, over-air-conditioned, cloyingly fragrant floors, where offerings ranged from Belgian chocolates and gourmet versions of traditional local snacks in the ground-floor food hall to fine china and baby booties on the penultimate level. The three of us stood in single file, one per moving step. Eyes fixed straight ahead, we ignored the advertisements featuring light-skinned, fair-haired, long-limbed beauties. Around us, the post-work crowd brisk-walked and jostled, talked loudly into cell phones and called out to people they knew. But we remained silent, the frenetic energy sinking into us like light into a black hole.

We'd been similarly laconic on the ride over. Ba opened his mouth only to warn us that this dinner was a big mistake, that involving more people — especially more Lins — would only complicate matters. In response, my mother, resplendent in a silk emerald-green blouse I hadn't seen her wear in years, reached out and touched her fingertips to my father's wrist, murmuring for him to stay calm. Maybe it was the color of her blouse, or the sumptuousness of the fabric, but her complexion had never looked so healthy, so bright. Despite all that had gone wrong earlier that day, and all that could go wrong still, prospects within my nuclear family, at least, seemed hopeful.

We stepped off the last escalator, and as we walked to the restaurant, I said, "Why are we even doing this? They know how you feel about Cal, and we know how they feel."

My father took my hand, his grip firm and reassuring as always. "Because Chinese families believe all problems can be solved over food."

Imperial Treasure was a low-ceilinged space filled with round, white-clothed tables of varying sizes and wooden chairs with swirling dragons carved into their backs. This nondescript décor was customary among the city's traditional Chinese restaurants, where ambience and service seemed intentionally halfhearted to highlight the care lavished upon the cuisine.

The restaurant manager, a small thick woman in a boxy black suit, hurried over. "Mr. and Mrs. Lin," she cried in Chinese. "*Lin xiao jie,*" she said, acknowledging me.

I smiled back.

"*Xian shen mei lai?*" the manager asked.

I kept smiling as I shook my head. No, my husband would not be joining us.

The manager led us to our private room, which was separated from the main dining area by a sliding door of fake mahogany panels. As we followed, she listed all the dishes Auntie Tina had ordered: crispy eel in sweet sauce, smoked duck two ways, hand-pulled noodles with crab roe — "luckily we had enough pregnant crabs on hand!" — and others I could not decipher from their poetic yet opaque Chinese names: squirrel-shaped Mandarin fish, eight treasure rice, four happiness pork.

A muscle flickered in Ba's jaw. Auntie Tina's extravagance seemed to anger him more. Ma tried to diffuse the tension by changing the subject. She asked the manager if we were among the first to arrive.

The manager gave a laugh that revealed the fillings in her back teeth. As a matter of fact, she said, we were the last to arrive. She pulled back the door with a flourish, and sure enough, the rest of the family was already seated around the large table.

Auntie Tina looked thinner and more anxious than she had a week earlier at the last family gathering, back when Uncle Robert was still pretending to support Ba's decision. Clearly the three of us had missed something important because my aunt was wringing her hands and shaking her head. Uncle Robert mopped his forehead with a handkerchief as Cal implored him to please, for once, just listen. Lily looked ready to burst into tears despite Rose's efforts to comfort her.

On the other side of the table, my cousins' spouses huddled together, relishing their noninvolvement. Rose's husband regarded the cell phone in his lap as he worked its buttons with both thumbs, no doubt playing some kind of computer game. Only Cal's wife, the kindest, most soft-spoken woman I knew, was by her husband's side. She sat all the way back in her chair, eyes ping-ponging from one family member to another and back again.

When we stepped through the doorway, the talking stopped. My father, my mother, and I took the three remaining seats. We unfurled our napkins from stiff white fans.

Seemingly oblivious to the tension in the room, the manager clapped her hands twice. "Now that everyone's here," she said cheerfully, "I'll have the kitchen send out the food." When no one said anything, she gave a quick nod and left.

The door shut firmly behind her, sealing out the noise from the main dining area. Inside our room, the silence was thick enough to wade through. Lily's husband contorted his face in slow motion, sneezed into his cupped hands and mumbled, "Scue me," and somehow, we all exhaled.

Cal's wife picked up her chopsticks, spun the lazy Susan, and began thrusting boiled peanuts—soaked in Lin's light soy sauce—at any plate within reach. Auntie Tina turned to my mother and asked how she was feeling. I combed through my aunt's words for any hint of judgment, and when I concluded she was sincere, I turned my attention to Rose, who'd launched into a story about her recent visit with the obstetrician: she'd actually seen her unborn baby girl stick out her tongue on the ultrasound monitor.

"It's the most amazing thing I've ever seen," Rose said. "Wasn't it amazing, Da-ling?" she swatted her husband, who was still staring down at his phone.

"What's that, Da-ling?" he asked, and then caught himself. "Yes, yes it was."

"I'll email you a picture," she said to me.

I tried to match my cousin's enthusiasm, though in truth, the blurry black-and-white ultrasound photographs my friends posted online always left me underwhelmed. Until he grew impatient with my indecisiveness, Paul and I had kept an ongoing list detailing the kind of parents we vowed never to become. I'd pitched boarding school as the key to healthy parent-child relations, to which he'd replied, "We'll see."

Two waiters glided into the room with trays of red wine glasses, prompting Cal to jump up to supervise the aerating of the Bordeaux he had selected from his personal collection—something he did to mark special occasions.

He instructed one waiter to distribute the glasses around the table, and handed the other a pair of handsome crystal decanters. "Yes," he said to the second waiter, who was clearly confused. "First, pour it in here, then later, we pour it in there."

As Cal leaned in to take a deep whiff of the wine, my shoulders shifted involuntarily toward my mother. In the midst of the chaos, I hadn't stopped to consider how Ma would react to being at a table of freely imbibing individuals.

Cal returned to his seat looking pleased. "'99 *Lafite*," he announced, shrugging in faux modesty.

Even I knew to be impressed.

My cousin couldn't resist looking straight at Ba and adding, "Uncle Xiong, I know it's your favorite."

Ba thanked him stiffly. Either he was in no mood to be charmed by Cal, or he too was worried about Ma.

Meanwhile, the waiters worked their way around the table in opposite directions, serving the decanted wine, getting closer and closer to my mother. My breath moved high up in my chest; I could not slow it down. Should I abstain in a gesture of solidarity? Would it only call more attention to Ma?

At last a waiter arrived at my side, and I signaled for a very small pour.

Beside me, Ma waved a palm over her glass. "None for me," she said softly.

Auntie Tina raised her eyebrows, but I didn't care. I had to fight the urge to throw my arms around my mother, to tell her how very proud I was.

With mild disdain the waiter plucked my mother's glass from the table, like a wilted rose in an otherwise perfect arrangement. I raised my glass and tried to drink as casually as possible. My father took a small sip. Around us, the rest of the family swirled and sniffed and swished and chewed.

Finally, Uncle Robert cleared his throat. "*Kor*," he said to Ba. "The boy has something he wants to say."

Auntie Tina pushed back her glass and interlaced her fingers as if saying a prayer. Rose's husband slid his phone into his breast pocket and exchanged looks with Lily's husband. My mother refilled her teacup.

Ba waited.

Cal brushed a thumb over his wedding band like it was some sort of good luck charm and took a long drink of his wine. When he began to speak, his face was calm, his eyes solemn and sincere. "Uncle Xiong—no, all of you." His gaze circled the table. "My family."

His mother dabbed a tissue to the corners of her eyes. His sisters made small, sympathetic noises. Even Ma refrained from whispering a snide remark.

Cal started again. "This past year, I was so thrilled with the new line of sauces. I'd finally made something from start to finish, all on my own."

I had to admit it was a good strategy—claiming that if he had any faults, it was only because he cared too much.

"But I got caught up in the excitement. I let my pride get in the way. I didn't take the time to examine all the necessary details. That was wrong."

My aunt choked back a sob.

Cal bit his lip. "Uncle Xiong," he said at last, "I know what Ah-kong and you and my dad have put into this company. I care about Lin's as much as you do. I've worked here my whole life." His voice cracked. For once he seemed unsure of himself. "I can do better. I will do better. Please." His voice trailed off.

All heads turned to Ba, who studied the place setting before him, as though expecting the answer to surface in that white ceramic plate. When he looked up he said, "Cal, I accept your apology."

Auntie Tina gasped. Lily and Rose traded small hopeful smiles.

"But I cannot change my mind," he said. "You can't come back. I'm sorry."

Everyone spoke at once, drowning out the rest of Ba's words.

"You can't be serious, *Kor*," said Uncle Robert. "He made a mistake. We all make mistakes."

"He's just a kid," Auntie Tina wailed.

And, "He's family. You can't get rid of family."

And, "Who do you think you are anyway?"

And, "Robert, you're the goddamned president. Do something!"

"Some mistakes have greater consequences than others," said Ma.

I thought I saw my parents' hands touch beneath the tablecloth.

The manager swept into the room, followed by a waiter bearing a porcelain tureen the size of a washtub. Everyone fell silent.

"Double-boiled fish soup. Compliments of master chef," the manager announced, her voice wavering when she noticed the distress on our faces. "The soup simmered for over twenty-four hours?" she added hopefully.

This dish was one of my favorites; I wished I hadn't lost my appetite.

The silence continued as the waiter ladled out milky broth, laden with plump slices of white cod and lacy curls of spring onion. Beads of sweat dotted his nose as he worked; the poor chap clearly couldn't wait to leave the room.

We dutifully dunked our soupspoons in the broth. Auntie Tina whispered in Uncle Robert's ear, and he grimaced and brushed aside whatever she'd said. Ba, too, picked up his spoon and began to eat. For a moment, the strangely hypnotic sounds of slurping were all we heard as each of us waited for someone else to make a move.

Ba continued to eat mechanically. In between bites he said, "Yes, everyone makes mistakes." A pause. "And, yes, every decision in-volves some element of risk." Another pause. He turned to Cal. "I want to make this very clear: You were fired not because you made a mistake. You were fired because you lied about it."

Cal's spoon landed in his bowl with a plop. "I was trying to take some initiative, to solve the problem myself," he said, but Ba held up his hand.

To Uncle Robert, Ba said, "You can't run a company with people you don't trust."

"He's my son," Uncle Robert said, and then he pulled back and switched tactics. "I can't run a company alone. We're in the middle of the biggest expansion Lin's has ever seen. Please, *Kor*. Give the boy a chance. Let him prove he's trustworthy."

Beside me, Ma shifted in her seat. She was attentive and alert, so different from previous family dinners. Typically, by this point in the meal, she'd be on her second or third glass, spewing forth a steady stream of sarcastic commentary that both amused and horri-fied me.

"All right?" she mouthed at me.

"All right," I mouthed back.

By now, nobody was eating, and the leftover twenty-four-hour double-boiled soup cooled in our bowls.

My aunt blew her nose into her tissue. "You're wrong about him, Xiong," she sniffed. "You're so, so wrong."

"Mummy, come on," Lily said, reaching across the table to press a hand to her mother's.

The sight of so many miserable faces seemed to weigh on Ba. "Look," he said. "Cal has done some excellent work. No one is questioning his dedication."

"Then, why?" asked Auntie Tina, drawing a warning look from her husband.

"Go on," Uncle Robert said.

Ba pressed his napkin to his lips. "Here's what I propose," he said. "Why not put Cal in charge of our real estate holdings?"

I wondered how long he'd been mulling over this solution.

To Cal, he said, "It'll be good for you to experience something besides soy sauce."

My cousin's fist hit the table so hard, my body recoiled. His wine glass toppled on its side, splashing *Chateau Lafite* '99 all over the starched white tablecloth and his wife's cream blouse.

"*Wie Schade*," my mother muttered, sounding like her old self. *What a shame.*

Cal leapt to his feet. "I've spent my entire adult life at Lin's. I'm the only one who put in the time." He gestured wildly to his sisters and to me. "Now you want to make me a glorified landlord?"

His wife dipped her napkin in her water glass and drew it across the long dark stain in the center of her sternum. "Oh, dear," she whispered. "Oh, dear."

"You must be crazy," Cal said to my father. "I would rather work for Yellow River."

"That's another option," Ba said quietly.

Cal's jaw hardened. He yanked on his wife's arm. "Come on. We're leaving."

"You better sit back down, Boy," said Uncle Robert.

"You can't leave," said Auntie Tina. "We have to resolve this."

I'd forgotten that here in Singapore, no matter your age, no matter your accomplishments, you'd always be "Boy" or "Girl" to your parents.

Indeed, Cal hesitated, perhaps reluctant to defy his parents in front of the whole family. But then he shook his head, almost in apology, and charged out of the room. His wife followed closely behind, nearly slamming into the two waiters who were standing by the door with the next course.

The waiters dropped the cast-iron platter and a stack of plates on the lazy Susan and rushed from the room without splitting the dish into individual portions. The crispy eel and leeks continued to sizzle and caramelize in the pool of hot peanut oil, and the intoxicating fragrance of sugar and fat filled the room. No one reached for a plate.

My uncle threw aside his napkin. "Listen to me, *Kor*. Cal's my son, and of course I want him at Lin's, but you also have to be practical, *mah*. We're not getting any younger."

And then my father played his final card. "What would our father have done?"

Uncle Robert's mouth fell open. It was clear he'd been caught off guard.

"What would Ba have done if one of us did what Cal did?"

Uncle Robert found his voice. "That's just it," he shouted in triumph, or desperation—it was hard to tell which. "Can't you see? That's just it. There are two of us, and there's only one of him."

Slowly, my father turned to me.

Before I could register what was happening, Ma spoke. "No," she said, raising an index finger. "Don't you dare. This company is not her problem."

"Her?" my aunt cried. "She just started. What could she possibly know?"

My uncle slapped the side of his head. "That's what this is all about?"

"Doesn't she have school?" asked Lily.

"Does she even want to stay?" asked Rose.

Ba's eyes locked onto mine. On his face was an expression I'd seen before. The voices around us faded, as if someone had reached for the volume knob and cranked it all the way down.

During those weekly childhood lessons, Ba had taught me about chemical hydrolysis, the process used to make the cheapest sauces. Ma's laugh rang out as she floated past, her arms laden with books. "You really think your six-year-old knows what you're talking about?" Ba placed his hand on top of my head and said, "She'll get it soon enough." And there was that expression: his eyes never wavering, his smile calm.

Uncle Robert reached out to grasp my father's forearm. He said, "Gretchen is welcome to stay as long as she wants. Hell, she can stay forever. But this isn't an either-or situation. Cal deserves another chance."

I wanted them to stop talking about me like I wasn't in the room, but the look on my father's face made me hold back. He sat there, saying nothing, watching me and waiting.

11

～

IN EARLY SEPTEMBER, as San Franciscans celebrate the first summer-like days of the year by baring their pasty limbs in cut-offs and sundresses, Chinese Singaporeans prepare for a very different kind of celebration: *Zhong Yuan Jie*, or the Hungry Ghost Festival.

On the seventh month of the lunar calendar, they say the gates of Hell fly open, freeing the souls of the departed to wander the Earth for the next thirty days. To nourish these starving spirits, the Chinese set out whole suckling pigs, braised ducks, mandarin oranges, and other delicacies. They burn offerings of joss sticks, fat wads of hell money and papier-mâché renderings of TVs, cars and jewelry, filling the air with sickly sweet smoke. They construct large outdoor stages for traditional Chinese puppet shows and operas, as well as contemporary song and dance performances—the latter presumably to appeal to the more recently departed souls. At each *getai* performance, the front row of seats is reserved for these guests-of-honor and must remain empty.

As a child, I observed these preparations from the passenger side of my mother's Mercedes as we drove past the government-subsidized housing estates. Occasionally, Ma would stop at the Lorong Mambong wet market, located in one of the larger estates, affording me a chance to get closer to the festivities. In those days the supermarket was strictly for packaged foods; the wet market was where everyone bought their fresh produce. While Ma haggled with vegetable and fish vendors who raised their prices because they could tell she wasn't from the neighborhood, I lost myself among boxes of intricate, papier-mâché Louis Vuitton handbags and Rolex watches — offerings fit for the chic, label-conscious ghost. Eventually, Ma took my arm and led me away, her impatience signaling her feelings toward silly superstitions.

Our family was staunchly secular. Aside from a small altar in the corner of Auntie Tina's living room, none of the Lin's paid attention to the festival, though I did notice my aunt's reluctance to let Lily and Rose swim in our pool at this time of year. Rose told me malicious spirits lurked in the water's depths, waiting to drown small children. At this, Ma rolled her eyes.

Even though I'd always observed *Zhong Yuan Jie* from a strictly anthropological perspective, this year, the significance of the time period was difficult to ignore. As Ba and Uncle Robert continued to debate what to do about Cal, each claimed to best understand what their late father would have wanted. In photographs on our office walls, Ahkong smiled benignly at us as he shook hands with the minster of trade and industry, tasted soybeans straight from the jar, held up Lin's very first bottle of soy sauce — in the same packaging we continued to use today. His eyes sparkled, his lips formed that familiar lopsided grin, and yet we all knew his other side. When he was alive, he rarely deployed his sternness on us grandchildren, but I'd seen him and Ba and Uncle Robert fall into heated arguments that only ended when Ahkong pounded his fist on the table and announced, "*Gao lor.*" Enough. The decision was made.

Now, however, with no one to step in and pound his fist, neither son would back down.

As the days passed with no compromise in sight, Ba postponed his retirement once again. He and Uncle Robert dealt with their frustration by working longer and harder. They started coming to work earlier and earlier, sometimes before the night watchman finished his shift. My uncle devoted himself to the Mama Poon deal, which was finally official. He scheduled conference calls on California time, prompting the Americans to ask admiringly if he ever slept. My father studied the research that Frankie and I had completed when we'd first taken over the US Expansion Project. He started to look for suitable American distribution channels for our premium sauces. For the first time since my homecoming, Ma insisted on driving herself to dialysis so Ba could focus on work, and when I offered to be her chauffeur, she cast a long look in Ba's direction and said, "He needs you more than I do."

Out on the office floor, rumors swirled that some kind of buyout was inevitable; if that failed, they said, Lin's would split in two. From time to time, my co-workers huddled together to debate which brother to pledge allegiance to. Frankie told me they competed to come up with names for the spin-off company: Lin's Soy Sauce Number One, Sibling Rivalry Soy Sauce.

Meanwhile, Frankie and I tried to keep busy, and so did Cal. All of us knew our work could prove to be meaningless, depending on which of our fathers prevailed. Somehow, Cal and I tacitly agreed to avoid mentioning the family dinner. He and I took pains to never end up in the same room alone, and when forced to converse, we were civil yet terse.

Then, one morning, my uncle brought a thick folder to Cal's office and told him to figure out how quickly Lin's could ship its first batch of fiberglass-aged sauce to California. My uncle left the door open, making it clear he had nothing to hide.

Less than an hour later, Ba knocked on my door. I braced myself, sure he would try once again to pressure me in to staying at Lin's, long-term. Instead he handed me a list of American specialty food importers who might be interested in our premium sauces. He wanted Frankie and me to contact the ones who'd be best for Lin's.

Just like that, the battle lines were drawn.

If Frankie wished she'd ended up on the other side, she kept that information to herself. She'd never witnessed a family feud of this magnitude, and each new development left her bewildered. I tried to assure her that Ba and Uncle Robert would reach a resolution, as they always did, though I too was beginning to worry that this feud would never end.

For now, we were glad to have some guidance. Frankie and I divided up our tasks and got started. I was drafting an introductory email to send to our future partners when a buzzing sound rose from my bottom desk drawer. I located my phone in my purse and identified the caller: James.

Twelve days had passed since our first and only date. Twelve days, during which I'd received four meager text messages, all responses to baldly desperate, trying-to-be-witty messages I'd sent first.

"Hey, what are you up to tonight?" was all he said when I answered.

I lowered my phone and stared at the screen, as though it could provide insight into James Santoso's perplexing mind. I returned the phone to my ear. "You have got to be kidding."

Frankie appeared in the doorway. "Kidding about what?"

I signaled for her to give me one minute, but when she kept standing there, I tried to continue my phone conversation without instantly revealing whom I was talking to.

I settled for, "Explain to me why it's so impossible for you to plan ahead."

His laugh was warm and gravelly. "Work's been crazy. My contractors are incompetent. The restaurant's two months behind schedule. I've barely had time to eat."

If not for Frankie, I would have asked how he'd found the time to practice his beach volleyball skills. But there she was, leaning against the wall with her arms crossed, tapping her foot against the floor.

"What do you need?" I asked Frankie, covering the mouthpiece.

She asked if I'd finished drawing up the spreadsheet she'd requested, and when I said I hadn't started, her face darkened.

"Hey," I said into the phone, pleased to have an excuse to hang up. "I have to go. I have work to do, too, you know." I tried not to look at Frankie's face.

"Have dinner with me tonight."

"Give me one good reason why."

"I haven't had a proper meal all week," he said. "And I want to see you."

"Fine," I said, sighing heavily.

When I put down the phone, Frankie said, "Who was that?"

I suspected she already knew. "James," I said nonchalantly. "Apparently he's been swamped with work."

"Oh, Gretch," she said.

My cheeks burned. "What?"

She bit her lip and ducked her head. "You should do whatever you want."

Something flared within me. "I am, and I will."

She reached out, closed the door, and came right up to my desk. "You don't have to drop everything the instant he calls."

"I'm not dropping anything," I said. "I don't exactly have a packed social calendar right now."

"Okay. Just get me the spreadsheet before you leave."

"Let's say tomorrow morning to be safe. I can't stay late tonight." I watched Frankie struggle to hide her irritation.

"This may be hard for you to fathom," she said, "but I actually want to do well at this job." She stood there, so full of self-righteousness, I couldn't help myself.

"Frankie," I said, "look around. Do you think anyone here really cares what you do?"

Her jaw dropped, and then she compressed her lips and shook her head. "Send it to me first thing in the morning," she said and whirled around.

I turned back to my computer, determined not to let her ruin my good mood. At five o'clock sharp, I went home to get ready for my date.

In the end, my efforts were wasted. As I was pulling out of my parents' driveway, James called. He said he was exhausted from another interminable day, so would I mind coming straight to his condo? Oh, and picking up dinner on the way?

I could have told him no. I could have slammed on the brakes and gone right back inside. But I did no such thing. I did everything he requested, and when he asked me to sleep over, I did that, too. Seeing James in any capacity was preferable to not seeing him at all. What's more, I needed to get out of my parents' home, away from my father's probing, disappointed gaze.

Ba had already paid the deposit to the conservatory; he knew I'd made up my mind. Still, each time I looked in his face, I saw all the ways I was letting him down. The first time I'd left, Cal had stepped in to fill my place. This time, no one would.

My guilt grew and metastasized, and soon I was skipping meals at home. I canceled Ma's piano lessons, thankful she was doing better and no longer needed constant supervision. I raced to James's condo every time he called. I didn't know what I'd done to increase my appeal, but suddenly he wanted to see me all the time. Sometimes I brought takeout; sometimes James and I grabbed a quick dinner at one of the small, mediocre eateries by his condo. Our conversations were pleasant yet hollow, much like the sex.

As I tiptoed through the house to grab a fresh change of clothes, as I drove the now-familiar route back and forth from James's, as my father continued to watch me without saying a word, the unrelenting tropical sun bore down upon me day after day. The same sun that nourished our soybeans and broke them down into our prized golden brew only sapped my strength. I felt doomed to spend the next four months treading water, running in place, accomplishing nothing.

● ● ●

Two weeks into the search for American distributors interested in our premium sauce, Frankie informed me that Cal needed her help on his project. She set a large pile of documents on my desk. "You don't mind, do you?" she asked. "Nobody cares what I do around here, anyway."

Once she was gone, I dropped the entire pile in my trash can, and then immediately crouched beneath my desk and lifted the papers out, hoping no one had seen me do it.

Amid those papers, a glossy bright green pamphlet caught my eye. How it had landed in Frankie's pile, I didn't know. The pamphlet promoted the Fourth Annual International Natural Foods Trade Show, which would take place the following month in San Francisco. I read through the entire pamphlet, and then flipped back to the beginning and read through it once more.

The trade show was to be held at a gigantic convention complex next to the Yerba Buena Gardens, a five-acre sanctuary plopped down in the heart of San Francisco's financial district. I kicked off my loafers beneath my desk, imagining the freshly trimmed grass, rough and cool, against the soles of my feet.

I was still studying the pamphlet when Shuting stopped by to deliver office supplies. "They send that every year," she said. "We never go."

"Thanks," I said distractedly. I slipped my feet back in my shoes.

By the end of the day, I'd written a proposal for why the Fourth Annual International Natural Foods Trade Show was the perfect place to introduce Lin's premium soy sauce to America, and why I would be the perfect person to take it there. Yes, a lot more work needed to be done before we'd be able to export our premium sauces on a large scale. Yes, we needed a more comprehensive understanding of the American market. But we had to start somewhere, and what better way to build contacts and explore options, especially with the Mama Poon deal underway.

Ba loved the idea, just as I knew he'd love any idea that involved me taking on more responsibility at Lin's. My uncle, however, balked. He argued that the trip was a waste of money, that it would take much more than a trade show to convince American consumers to buy our premium sauces.

In the end, however, Uncle Robert agreed to send me to the show—mostly, I guessed, because he realized he'd have a better chance of changing Ba's mind about Cal while I was gone.

Only Frankie remained skeptical.

Later that day, she pulled me in her office. "Have you thought this through? Are you sure you're ready to see him?"

"Who?" I asked, hedging for time. The cardboard boxes of documents stacked high in the corner lurked like an unwanted guest.

She rolled her eyes.

"You mean Paul?" I said.

She blew a puff of air through her lips to show her exasperation. "Gretch, what are you doing?"

I said I didn't know what she meant.

"James told Pierre you're over at his place almost every night."

"You and your crew must really be hurting for things to talk about," I said, secretly flattered that James was discussing me with his friends. I wondered what else he'd told Pierre.

She ignored me. "I'm serious."

"Frankie," I said. "I'm going to a trade show. I need to start looking for an apartment in San Francisco. That's all there is to it. It's not a big deal."

"That's it?" she asked, her vehemence catching me off guard. Before I could respond, she said, "If this thing with James is so casual" — how she'd arrived at that conclusion I didn't get a chance to ask — "why do you blow off all your friends to be with him?"

Her long-lashed brown eyes were the eyes of my old college roommate, the girl who'd never had a boyfriend, the girl who couldn't get a date. "Okay," I said. "This isn't about me."

Her eyes narrowed. "What do you mean?"

I said, "I'm sorry nothing's changed for you. I'm sorry you came all this way only to remain single. You get asked out all the time. What are you afraid of?"

Frankie wrapped her arms around herself like she'd suddenly grown cold. When she spoke her voice was strained. "This has nothing to do with that."

"Oh really?" I asked, triumphant. "What's it about then? Go on, tell me."

She fixed her gaze on me, and I felt my bravado fade.

"Fine," she said. "Moving back to San Francisco is a mistake. He'll break your heart all over again."

Heat spread through my chest like a stain. I said, "You may recall that I have a master's program to complete."

Her face softened. "Look," she said, "I just — "

I cut her off. "No. You listen to me. I'm going back to San Francisco because that's my home now. You don't have a family like mine. You don't understand."

"So, you admit it," she said, her voice rising. "You're running away."

I slapped a palm on the table. A box of paperclips spilled on the floor. "Aren't you doing the same thing? Isn't that why you're here, halfway across the world? To escape all the people who know you used to be fat?"

Abruptly she bent over to retrieve the paperclips, one by one.

"Frankie," I said, but she didn't get up.

Even though Frankie was from Fresno, three hours away from Stanford, I'd been to her home only once, when we'd stopped to see her mother on our way to Los Angeles for spring break. Frankie's mom was tall and wide. Beneath her loose cotton housedress, she was soft and slouchy, the way Frankie used to be. Her mom served us grilled cheese sandwiches made with pre-sliced white bread and tomato soup from a can. After less than an hour, Frankie said we had to get going to avoid traffic, and her mom sent us off with a bag of marshmallows and a brave smile. In the car, Frankie said quietly, "Thanks. I'm sorry we had to do that." "You're most welcome," I said brightly, unsure of what else to add.

I knew how I must have seemed to Frankie: a spoiled, childish girl who took her family and friends for granted.

Frankie straightened and released a handful of paperclips on her desk. She dropped her palm to her lap with a defeated slap. "I guess we're both running away," she said.

I wanted to acknowledge that my denial was more serious than hers—I could at least give her that. But she closed her eyes, leaned her head against the back of her chair and said, "Can you really imagine spending the rest of your life in San Francisco?"

I was about to answer, but she continued, "Because sometimes I think I could do that here."

Her confessional tone surprised me. All my adult life I'd assumed I would settle in America, and yet Frankie's reservations made me backtrack. I couldn't recall if there was a point when I'd actually made my decision, or if I'd simply always known, and for the first time the distinction mattered.

"Really?" I asked. "Here? In tiny, claustrophobic Singapore?"

She said, "Isn't it crazy? I can't get over how crazy it sounds."

It was mid-September, and outside the window, along these hallways, presumably right here in the room, hungry ghosts roamed, transforming our earthly world into their own vast playground.

Soon, the festival would be over. The ghosts would return to the underworld, where they would remain, neglected by their descendants, until the following year. I did not believe in ghosts, I did not believe in life after death, but still I imagined Ahkong, trim in his short-sleeved shirt and tie, floating among us. His sons, they were not speaking; his grandson would admit no wrongs; his granddaughter prepared, once again, to flee. And in the meantime, she hid and ducked and looked away, in the hopes that by refusing to see the problems, she could absolve herself of blame.

12

NOT LONG AFTER I LAUNCHED my campaign to attend the trade show, on a night when James said he was too wiped out to see me, I went to my parents' bathroom in search of a Band-Aid, reached for Ma's toothbrush mug to get a drink of water, and caught a whiff of gin.

She insisted I was overreacting. It had only been a few sips. She'd needed a little help falling asleep. I was reading too much into the mug.

Each of her excuses threatened to send me crashing to my knees. My head was too heavy to hold up; I couldn't find my balance. I turned to Ba, but he was as stunned as I was.

Ma squared her shoulders. "One little slip-up can't invalidate all the progress I've made. I'm doing so much better, you both said so yourselves."

I moved around her and threw open the doors of the medicine cabinet.

"What do you think you're doing?" she said.

I charged around the bathroom, opening cabinets and drawers, and then I went in the bedroom and did the same.

"Stop," she screamed. "Stop it right now."

My father followed helplessly behind her.

There were bottles everywhere, some empty, some not: nestled among face creams and ointments, hidden in shoeboxes, wrapped in silk scarves.

"You made me do this," Ma said. "You forced this upon me."

I dragged my father from the room. "Please," I said, "we have to."

At first Ba closed his eyes and shook his head so abruptly it was almost a shudder. But then he whispered, "Okay."

His capitulation was so sudden, so complete, that if I'd had any lingering doubts before, I knew then, unequivocally, that all three of us were lost.

Later, I couldn't stop thinking about the series of events that had led me to Ma's bathroom: the razor that slipped from my soapy fingers, the empty Band-Aid box in my own dresser drawer. Was it really thirst or was it a familiar tingling in my nostrils that made me reach for that mug?

The Light on Life Rehabilitation Center was located on the northern tip of the island. During the entire drive over, Ma was on her best behavior. She was rational, composed.

She argued that she deserved another chance. "You've seen the statistics. These things rarely work the first time around."

The more sense she made, the tenser I grew.

When we arrived at the center, we were greeted by a series of picturesque Balinese open-air houses, lined with hibiscus bushes bursting with riotous, saucer-sized blooms. Eager to show how reasonable she was, Ma submitted to a medical examination, while Ba and I met with the director of the center, a longhaired, deeply tanned Australian, who looked more like a surf instructor or a river-rafting guide. He told us Light on Life practiced a 12-step-style program with a "holistic, secular twist."

"We're here to help our clients meet their goals, whatever that may mean," he said.

A look of mild terror settled on my father's face.

The director continued. "A client's goal could be abstinence. It could be drinking in moderation. We have no hard and fast rules."

He said other things I didn't register; I kept losing myself in the movement of his lips and teeth. Unlike Ba, I felt strangely calm. What mattered most was that Ma was out of the house with all of its hiding places, and in the hands of people more capable than myself.

"How do we check her in?" I asked.

When the meeting was over, we went to see Ma. Arms akimbo, chin raised, she stood in the center of the small, spare bedroom that would be her home for the next twenty-one days. They'd put her in an oversized white spa robe with Light on Life embroidered across its upper-right side. On Ma's tiny frame, the words sat awkwardly over her diaphragm and the robe's hem brushed her ankles.

"This whole thing is absurd. Take me home." She knew we would not leave her here against her will.

I waited for my father to say something wise and comforting, but all he managed was, "I'm sorry, Ling." He dropped his hands to his sides and hung his head. The thinning silver hair at the center of his crown revealed a swirl of pink scalp.

"Please, Ma, give it a try," I said. "We all need help." I nudged my father, willing him to back me up.

He said, "I don't know what to do. Ling, tell me what you want me to do."

She stood still as a statue in that too-large white robe. When she exhaled, her body receded into itself as though it wanted nothing more to do with us. Then she walked out on the tiny balcony, just large enough to fit a wooden folding chair.

"We love you," I said. "We'll be back tomorrow." I stepped forward to hug my mother, but she slid shut the balcony door and did not look back.

I don't know how long my father and I stood there, waiting for Ma to acknowledge us. When I finally faced him, he looked so stricken I knew I had to get him out of there.

I said, "She needs time to be alone. Tomorrow will be a better day." I took his hand to lead him out, and his fingers clung to mine.

That first week, Ba and I visited Ma every day after work. We tried to engage her, recounting the latest news from Lin's, but she ignored us, sometimes even leaving the room.

Afterward, Ba and I followed the winding flagstone path to the parking lot—one last brief stretch of amity before we got in our respective cars and went our separate ways.

Only once did Ba ask where I was going.

"To dinner," I answered, my pulse leaping into double time. We'd never actually spoken about James.

"And when will you come home?"

The sun hung low in the sky and a cool breeze rustled the trees, but my face grew hot. I began to sweat. "I haven't decided."

Ba maintained the same brisk pace, and I'd never felt so happy to see my car come into view. "This is me," I said dumbly. I pressed the button on my key to unlock the doors, and the car emitted a cheerful beep.

Ba stopped, blocking my path to the driver's seat. "You're never too old to make stupid decisions," he said. "Look, I made the decision to take Ma to this place."

It seemed I would once again narrowly avoid having to discuss James. "Come on, Ba. They told us the first few days would be the worst."

He took a few steps back, giving me just enough room to squeeze past. "I want you to know, I don't blame you. It's my fault for listening."

I didn't try to defend myself. I didn't even move. "Do you want me to come home?"

He was already walking away.

"I mean, right now?" I called after him.

He barely looked back; I couldn't read the expression on his face.

"Do whatever you want," he said. "It doesn't matter what I think."

After that, Ba and I took turns visiting my mother.

On alternate nights, I left the office right at five to make the center's visiting hours. Often I found my mother reading in her room with the balcony door ajar. I took this as a positive sign, even if she refused to look up from the pages. Perching on a folding chair across from her with a magazine of my own, I spent most of the time willing her to make eye contact, marveling at the energy it must have taken for her to so completely shut me out.

Her counselor assured me that this behavior was normal. Of

course, initially, my mother would feel angry, betrayed. The counselor told me to picture a wave coming right at me. That was the urge to drink. In the moment the wave peaked, you were sure it would sweep you off your feet, engulf you, drown you. But if you braced yourself and faced it straight on, the wave would pass. You would emerge on the other side. "Try to understand what your mother is going through," he said.

What I understood was this: as Ma worked to eliminate alcohol from her life, I was drinking more than ever. I'd become a permanent fixture at Chaplin's, where I downed one vodka tonic after another, waiting for James to return my calls, making up excuses to avoid my friends.

"You're a mess," Kat said when I finally agreed to meet her for dinner at an Italian restaurant by her office. "I mean, I know things aren't easy for you right now, but you are a mess."

My hand shot up to my greasy, unwashed hair. I saw no point in primping if I wasn't going to see James. I pressed my fingers to my eyelids and reveled for a moment in the darkness. "Thanks. And you wonder why I never want to come out."

"I know exactly why you're too busy to come out," she said, her voice razor sharp. She stabbed her fork in a mound of linguine and twirled.

"Kat," I said, "I really don't need relationship advice right now."

She finished chewing. "I was talking about your mother."

We both knew this was a lie. "But since you brought it up," I said, "we just checked my mother into rehab, and now she isn't speaking to us." I wasn't entirely sure why I'd chosen this moment to reveal the news, or why my voice was filled with spite.

Kat clamped a hand over her mouth. "Gretch, I'm sorry. How are you and your dad holding up?"

I told her I was fine, and as far as I knew, he was fine, too. Everyone was doing just fine.

She set down her fork. "Why is it so impossible for us to have a conversation?"

I pushed away my plate, my appetite gone. "How can I tell you anything when all you do is judge me?"

"So now I'm not allowed to show concern?"

I said, "Why don't you just say it? You think I'm a bad daughter. You think I choose men who treat me like shit."

"I'm worried about you," she said evenly. "You're not a bad daughter."

"Can you imagine what it's like to lose your husband?"

"I'm trying to understand. Help me understand," she said.

How could I tell her that even though Paul had cheated on me and left me, I would take him back? How could I explain why I clung to James? How could I say all this to Kat and expect her to feel anything but pity?

We ate quickly and paid the bill.

"Call me when you're ready to talk," Kat said, to which I said nothing at all.

Back at my parents' house, I sliced open the cardboard box of books I needed to read or re-read before beginning my thesis semester in January. I emailed the same brave, lighthearted update to Marie, Andrea, and Jenny at the conservatory, reaching out to them for the first time since leaving San Francisco. Given Ma's fragile state, I held off on planning my trip to the trade show. Still, I searched online apartment listings for studios and small one bedrooms with good light, wood floors, gas stoves. And even though I jumped each time James called, I spent more and more time day dreaming about Paul. I imagined running into him outside our old neighborhood coffee shop or at our favorite taqueria in the Mission or simply on the street somewhere in our city. "I didn't realize you were back," he would say, coming toward me with outstretched arms. Coolly, I would reply, "There's no reason you would."

Nights, I lay awake in bed, my mind racing through everything I needed to do before I left Singapore, and everything that awaited me in San Francisco. When sleep truly escaped me, I reached over to my nightstand, turned my metronome to forty, the slowest setting, and counted the steady clicks. Once the needle got going, all you had to do was keep time.

Halfway through Ma's second week, I asked Frankie to come with me to the rehab center. I couldn't bear the thought of spending another evening staring at my mother's stony face, or over the balcony at the condo complex emerging slowly but surely through the distant treetops. I'd sipped endless Styrofoam cups of watered-down Lipton tea from the giant thermos in the waiting room. I was desperate. Frankie and Ma had met several times over the years, and had always enjoyed each other's company.

"Gretch," Frankie said, "I had no idea."

I felt a pang of affection for Kat, who'd kept the news to herself. "So, you'll come?"

Perhaps Frankie saw my invitation as a gesture of goodwill; perhaps she simply felt sorry for me. At any rate, she agreed to come.

After work, we took the Bukit Timah Expressway, passing the

reservoirs and nature reserves in the very center of the island. Just east of the factory, just west of the central business district, the greenery was almost blindingly lush. When we stepped out of the car, the air was startling in its stillness, untainted by the whirring motors and ringing cell phones and low, electric drone that formed the backbone of this city.

As I scribbled our names on the visitor sign-in sheet, the receptionist, a young Malay woman in a purple floral headscarf gazed at Frankie with interest. "Are you from US?"

Frankie ducked her head and muttered, "Yes." She knew to be wary.

"Which part?" the receptionist persisted. "New York?"

I'd walked past this woman at least a dozen times. While she'd never been rude, she'd never spoken to me before.

"California," said Frankie.

The receptionist nodded knowingly, as though that would have been her second guess. "How lovely. I hear it's nice there."

At Lin's our co-workers had gotten used to Frankie, and I'd forgotten that elsewhere she attracted this kind of attention every day. All over Singapore, shopkeepers, security guards, taxi drivers watched her with interest. Over half a century removed from British colonial rule, our nation's lingering fascination with the West manifested itself in larger-than-life billboards of Caucasian and Eurasian models, in local newscasters' approximations of the Queen's English, in whole airplanes filled with students heading to universities abroad. Once, at a bus stop, a group of teenage girls wanted to know if Frankie was a certain Australian actress. When Frankie blushed and shook her head, they huddled together and erupted into giggles. Nothing remotely similar ever happened to me in San Francisco, where, if anything, I prided myself on blending in.

Now I led Frankie down the corridor to my mother's room, "Don't be surprised if she flips out."

Frankie assured me she was prepared.

Ma was on her balcony, reading, her back to us. When she turned, the book fell from her hands.

"Ma, I brought a friend."

Ma hurried to us. "Frankie Shepherd," she said. "You look stunning." I couldn't believe she was actually speaking, if not directly to me. And then, for the first time since the morning we'd left her in this room, Ma looked straight at me and said, "Why didn't you tell me you were bringing Frankie? I would have tidied up." Her hand fluttered up to her fully made-up face, the subtly rouged cheeks and penciled-in brows. The room was spotless, the turned-back edge of the white cotton blanket on the twin bed the only clue of inhabitance.

I wanted to wrap my arms around Ma, and then around Frankie, who had already leaned in to hug my mother. "It's so good to see you, Mrs. Lin."

"No need so formal, *lah*," Ma said, who only used Singlish with people who were in on the joke. "Call me Ling. Or since you're Singaporean now, Auntie Ling."

"Auntie Ling," Frankie repeated.

Ma sat herself on the edge of the bed and gestured to a chair. "Sit," she said to Frankie. "It's good to see you after all these years, even in this unfortunate setting."

Frankie gazed out the balcony's sliding door. "But what a wonderful view."

"It's a regular Ritz-Carlton. My husband and daughter would settle for nothing less."

I stiffened, unable to measure the malice in her tone, but then Ma said, "As far as these places go, this one isn't so bad. Or so I've heard."

The backs of my eyes began to smart. I couldn't help myself.

My mother turned to Frankie and said, "Tell me everything. How are you liking Singapore this time around? I'm sorry we missed you when you were last here. And how is Lin's? You certainly showed up at an interesting time."

When Frankie began to tell her about work, I slipped out the door to fetch us all some tea.

Lingering in the corridor, I peered in an airy, high-ceilinged room, where a half-dozen ladies and a single, older potbellied man strained their stiff, lumpy bodies into a basic yoga pose. The instructor was young and taut with short, spiky hair. She radiated such health and wellness that here, among the patients, her presence stung like a well-placed slap. Out in the Japanese garden by the fishpond, a painfully slight girl with bruised arms threw chunks of bread at fat orange carp, while a graying middle-aged couple — her parents? — looked on. Some of these patients would stay for up to a year, while my mother was already halfway through her three-week tenure. I didn't need her counselor to warn me that relapses were common. He told me he himself had relapsed twice before finally staying sober. Proudly he said that his ten-year "sober birthday" would fall on the following month.

Disappointment, heartbreak flowed through corridors, connecting these spacious rooms, and yet all these people kept stretching, straining, striving. America's favorite talk show host's plush voice filled my ears: "You will get better because you are here." As if things could be so simple.

I returned to the room with three cups of tea on a plastic tray.

My mother was listing movie stars in an attempt to uncover the kind of man Frankie hoped to date. "Brad Pitt," she said. "Colin Firth. Mark Ruffalo. Who's that young guy? Adrian Grenier. I can see you with someone like him."

Frankie giggled and shook her head.

I handed them their tea; they thanked me absently.

"None of these?" Ma asked in disbelief.

When I expressed admiration for her familiarity with Hollywood's leading men, Ma pointed out she'd spent nearly three decades surrounded by undergrads. Indeed, she'd won the university teaching award so many years in a row, her colleagues used to joke that the administration should fold the prize money into her salary and forgo the annual announcement. Now I wondered about her students, the ones whose A-level scores were too low to read law, the ones who couldn't afford to go abroad. How they must have missed my mother.

Ma turned her attention back to Frankie. "So there's nobody special right now? I find that hard to believe."

"That's the problem," Frankie said, throwing up her arms. "I've barely dated at all. I don't know where to start."

Ma pursed her lips, and Frankie went on. "It gets worse every year. Soon I'll be the thirty-one-year-old, or thirty-two-year-old, or forty-year-old who's never had a boyfriend. I hate first dates. When I tell the truth about my past relationships — or lack thereof — the guy always looks at me like I'm some sort of freak."

She'd told me all this before, and I never knew what to say, except a version of, "You just need to meet the right guy. He'll understand."

My mother took Frankie's hand. "For one thing," she said, "everybody hates first dates." She said it with such conviction I momentarily forgot how many decades had passed since her last first date. She continued, "If the only issue is your lack of experience, then for Christ's sake, just lie."

There was a moment of stunned silence, and then the laughter streamed out of us, Frankie and me.

Ma looked pleased. "Better yet," she said. "Tell those nosy men it's none of their business. Let them think your past is more checkered than it is."

Frankie grew serious. "You're right. That's a great strategy."

Ma squeezed Frankie's hand, and something swelled inside me. I had so much I wanted to discuss with my mother, so many questions on my mind. If our relationship had been different, if I'd been as truthful and open with Ma as she'd always tried to be with me, what words of wisdom would she have shared?

At the end of the hour, Ma took Frankie in her arms and told her to come back and visit anytime. Then she reached for me, and I hugged her back with all my might until she laughed and said, "But I'll see you day after tomorrow."

Out in the waiting room, I clasped Frankie's arms. "Thank you. I haven't seen her that happy in so long."

"Thanks for bringing me," she said. "And thanks to Auntie Ling, I might actually get some action now." She undid her ponytail and shook out her hair, and I asked where she was heading off to this evening.

"I'm having drinks with some girls I met by the condo pool. Want to come?"

"Can't tonight," I said, as though I would have said yes at any other time.

"Next time, then," she said.

The receptionist in the purple floral headscarf waved as we stepped out the door.

Out on the curb, we hugged good-bye, and Frankie said, "Have fun with James."

Something in her delivery begged for a response, but I didn't answer. Grateful as I was for Frankie's support this evening, I didn't need to justify my decisions to her.

I was already in the car before I noticed I'd left my cell phone in Ma's room. I hurried back to the center and was surprised to find my mother in bed with the covers pulled up to her chin.

"What are you doing back here?" She struggled to sit up.

"Are you feeling okay? Do you want me to get a nurse? Should I stay?" I retrieved my phone from the nightstand and slipped it in my purse.

"Nonsense. Of course not." She fluffed up her pillow and set it beneath her lumbar region.

I eyed the door and then immediately felt guilty. I took a step toward her. "I'm sorry it had to happen this way," I said.

She pushed down the covers. "I didn't make it easy for you."

"Are you sure you're okay?" What I truly wanted to know, I couldn't put into words.

She brushed away my question with one of her own. "What's this trip you have planned?"

I grew very still. "Frankie told you?"

Ma nodded, and I wondered if Frankie had also shared her thoughts on Paul.

"Don't worry," I said. "I'm not going anywhere. Not with you here."

With a perfectly polished finger, Ma beckoned me close. "Listen to me. Go find yourself an apartment in San Francisco. Go back to living your life."

I took a step back, banging my hip on a folding chair.

Ma's eyes gleamed. "You've wasted enough time here."

"Ma," I said. "You have to get better."

"I'm telling you to go." Sitting up in that pristine white bed, she looked calm and reasonable and perfectly in control.

Somewhere outside the room, a staff member rang a bell, signaling the end of visiting hours.

"We'll discuss this some other time," I said, and she arced her brows and gave me a pointed look. But when I leaned in to kiss her, she turned her head and kissed me firmly back, leaving a faint lipstick imprint on my cheek that I wouldn't notice until later.

The door to James's condo was open.

"Come on in," he called from the kitchen.

Of course I knew he liked to cook; he'd practically grown up in his family's restaurants. Still, when he'd mentioned earlier that he felt like making dinner, my heart had soared. Why now? Why was he putting in all this effort when I was getting used to his careless approach to dating?

I found James standing in front of the shiny, commercial-grade range, tending a large copper pan into which he tossed a handful of minced garlic, light and fine as wedding confetti. The garlic landed with a sizzle, and pungent smoke billowed in the air. James batted it away from the smoke detector with an oven mitt.

I waited for him to stop flailing his arms before closing the distance between us. He was the kind of guy who always smelled clean, even when he was sweating over a pan of garlic. I tongued the slick skin on his neck, and he glanced back, surprised, then let me peck him on the mouth.

On the menu were a fennel and orange salad, orecchiette with kale and Italian sausage, and chocolate ice cream for dessert. He described this last course somewhat sheepishly—the ice cream was store bought. I found this so adorable that I reached around, pinched his cheek, and was promptly banished from the kitchen.

The dining room's parquet floor was smooth and cool against my bare feet. I helped myself to a lightly chilled bottle of pinot noir, and then folded my legs into a roomy cream-colored leather chair. From this vantage point, I watched as James chopped and tossed and flipped with ease.

Throughout my childhood, my father had been in charge of Sunday dinner, on the maid's one day off. He'd sit me on the counter, far enough away from the hot pans to avoid sauce spatters, but close enough so he could reach over and give me a taste from his wide wooden spatula. When he made my favorite *bak kut teh,* a fragrant, spicy soup with tender pork spare ribs and fat shitake mushrooms, he always had me sample the stock. He taught me to make a big slurping sound as I sipped to avoid burning my tongue. He taught me to discern the warmth of cinnamon, the tang of orange peel, and the mellow licorice of star anise. Most importantly, Ba taught me to appreciate the way a dash of Lin's light soy sauce brightened each of these flavors while pulling them together into a single, harmonious whole.

Earlier in the year, before my cousin's disaster, during Ba's first attempt at retirement, he'd talked about taking a French cooking class. He'd always been interested in incorporating soy sauce into Western cuisine. After all, real soy sauce was so much more complex and flavorful than plain old table salt. These days, however, when the maid was off, Ba ate out, or picked up prepared food from the grocery store. He was working more than ever; who knew when he'd have time to cook again?

In the kitchen, James worked, the muscles in his back and shoulders rippling beneath his thin T-shirt. I let myself imagine that this was my life: coming home from a day at the office to a handsome man, a glass of wine, a home-cooked meal; my family a short drive away.

But now that I had Ma's approval, I was going to the trade show, and I had to tell James. I had no idea what I'd say when he asked if I was planning to see Paul.

"How's work?" he called over his shoulder.

I took a deep breath. "Did I tell you I'm going to San Francisco next week?"

"Oh, yeah? What for?"

I told him about the trade show.

"Cool," he said. He emerged from the kitchen with two large serving bowls. "Hope you're hungry." He set the bowls on the table and reached for the wine. "Is this any good?" He turned the bottle so he could read the label.

I told him it was, and waited for the inevitable question.

He poured himself a glass, dug a serving spoon in the salad bowl, plopped a large mass on his plate, and pushed the bowl over to me. "It's been ages since I've done this," he said.

I took a small bite. "It's delicious."

"Yeah, not bad." He served himself some pasta, and began to eat that. "Could use a touch more salt, don't you think?" he asked, not noticing that I had yet to move on from my salad.

When he returned with the saltshaker, I said, "Listen, I haven't made plans or anything, but I'm probably going to see my ex."

He looked at me blankly.

"In San Francisco."

He nodded. "Makes sense."

I waited for him to say more, and when he didn't, I said, "I'm glad you're okay with this."

A hint of smugness played in the edges of his smile. "Why wouldn't I be?"

I chewed my orecchiette and swallowed without tasting it. "Oh, I don't know," I said. "Most couples — most people who've been seeing each other like we have would probably want to discuss if one of the people was going to see his or her ex."

James watched me, amused. "Okay. What do you want to discuss?"

"Forget it."

He took a sip of wine and wiped his mouth. "No, really, let's talk about it."

"No, let's not." I laughed unconvincingly. "How silly of me to think you'd find this worth discussing."

The smug smile vanished. "Let's not play this game. If there's something you want to say, go for it. We're both adults."

I released my fork with a clang. "Adults?" I repeated. "I'm not the one who wants to get laid every night, but can't stand the thought of being attached in any way. I'm not the one behaving like a teenage boy."

He held up both palms. "Hang on, Gretchen. You're the one who's leaving in January."

I looked away, fighting to quiet the voices in my head: but he hadn't asked me to stay. Not that I would have stayed anyway. Why did he have the upper hand when I was the one leaving? Why was I trying to make this relationship something it wasn't?

Already the adrenaline was draining out of me. I wondered what I could say to salvage the evening. The pasta had begun to congeal on my plate, taking on a grayish cast. I took a bite and said, "Yum."

"Gretchen," James said.

"Yes?" I asked hopefully.

"I don't know what you want from me."

"I'm sorry I said anything. Let's just enjoy this amazing dinner you made."

He shook his head. "Maybe it's best if you go."

"Right now?"

"Right now."

I waited for him to change his mind, and when he remained silent, I pushed back my chair, scraping the chair legs against the parquet floor. I stalked into the living room to retrieve my purse. "So, that's it? You're kicking me out?"

He filled his wine glass to the brim, and I imagined tipping the remaining pinot noir all over his pristine cream-leather upholstery.

He moved the bottle out of my reach. "I guess I am."

"Well," I said. "Thank you for a lovely evening."

He didn't get up from the table. "Good-bye, Gretchen," he said.

13

PAUL: JUST A HEADS-UP that I'm going to be in SF next week. Would be great to see you. Otherwise, hope you're well! — Gretch

HOW I'D MULLED over these lines, swapping out the final exclamation point for a period, then changing it back again. I was going for casual and breezy, though I felt anything but.

Hours, then days passed with no response. As the morning of my flight drew near, I busied myself with preparations: printing up posters, pamphlets and business cards for the trade show, lining up apartment viewings, making plans to see Marie, Andrea, and Jenny.

The more I tried to convince myself I wasn't waiting for a response, the more I checked my cell phone, hit the refresh button on my email and re-read my most recent exchanges with Paul for clues to his silence. Once or twice, I found myself wide awake in the middle of the night, unable to fall back to sleep before checking my email one last time. Not only was there never anything from Paul, there were no other messages either — not from Kat, James, or even Frankie.

The night before my flight, I was still at work when I discovered that the hotel where Shuting swore she'd booked my room had mysteriously lost the reservation. I'd planned to visit Ma at the center, but now I had to scramble to find something within walking distance from the convention hall.

Frankie stopped by my office to say good-bye, and when I explained why I was so frazzled, she said, "Want me to go? I'm always up for hanging out with Auntie Ling."

I handed over the metronome I'd been meaning to take to Ma ever since we'd discovered the out-of-tune piano in the center's yoga room. "She needs to practice while I'm gone," I explained to Frankie. "Tell her it doesn't matter how fast or how slow as long as she keeps time."

Frankie cocked her head and smiled. "Don't worry. Everything will be fine here."

I noticed she didn't offer any reassurance about what would happen in San Francisco.

That night, I was in my bedroom, packing my suitcase, when I heard a knock on the door. My father stood in the doorway, a solemn expression on his face as he watched me fold and refold a thin ribbed cardigan.

"Are you ready for tomorrow?" he asked.

I told him I was.

"I want to talk to you."

I waited.

"This is a good thing you're doing, taking our sauce to America."

"Thanks, Ba," I said, the guilt already pooling in my belly.

"And I think it's a worthwhile way to spend your last few months as part of Lin's."

"I'll do my best," I said.

"Good," Ba said, his gaze scanning the room. "Good."

I hoped we'd reached the end of the conversation, but he cleared his throat, a strange look in his eyes. "A wound is a funny thing," he began.

I didn't follow. "A what?"

"A wound, like an injury, a pain, *lah*," he said impatiently.

"Oh."

That brief outburst seemed to set him at ease. He told me to picture a knife plunged in flesh. Initially the pain was excruciating, enough to make the wounded person give up altogether. With time, however, the wound healed around the knife; the wounded person could live in more or less tolerable discomfort. In fact, more pain would be caused by removing the knife completely and forcing the wound to heal anew.

"Do you know what I'm talking about, Xiao Xi?" he asked. Something about the way he said my name made my tear ducts well.

I told him I did, once again hoping to end the conversation. Despite his efforts to connect, I was too intoxicated by the promise of my trip to focus on what he was trying to say.

Before he left, Ba said, "I know you will do fine." There again was that steady gaze. Like my mother, he was so sure of himself, so sure of what was in store for me.

One pushed me to return to America, the other urged me to pull out the knife, let the wound heal, and remain in Singapore. But I was done choosing sides, pleasing one over the other. From here on out, I would find a way to please myself.

"Good," I could hear Ma say now. "All I ever wanted was for you to have a choice."

Ba would jump in. "The decision is always yours, what. But you must consider the full range of option."

"*Options,*" said Ma.

I banished their voices from my head, if only for a moment's peace.

14

THE SINGAPORE AIRLINES BOEING 747 touched down in San Francisco on an unseasonably cold, gray, October afternoon. An afternoon shrouded in rain so fine, droplets didn't fall so much as seep through the seams of my coat.

Despite my jet lag, I wound a scarf around my neck, pulled up my waterproof hood and went to see a potential apartment, a tiny studio in Russian Hill, not far from the apartment Paul and I had shared. The studio boasted a cracked bathtub and thick brown wall-to-wall carpeting that appeared to have been installed in the seventies. My mother's look of horror flashed in my mind—a look so exaggerated it was almost cartoon-like. And then I remembered she would probably never again make the trip to San Francisco. In four days, she'd be released from the Light on Life Rehabilitation Center, only to be confined to a country traversable in under an hour.

The next two apartments were no better, and fatigue didn't help my mood.

Several hours remained before I was scheduled to meet my classmates for drinks near the conservatory. Most of that time I spent telling myself how good it was to be back, even as I tried to remember if the fog had always been so white and so thick, if the public buses had always run so infrequently, if the neglected and the wounded had always monopolized sidewalks and park benches. The pink and green Victorians I'd once found so charming now leered at me like overpainted working girls. Every neighborhood felt gritty, every apartment too expensive and cramped.

Over eight-dollar Belgian beers, my classmates asked how I was spending my semester off.

"Aside from work, family, the usual stuff, I've watched a lot of TV—mainly *Melody* re-runs. She's incredibly popular in Singapore." Topics I didn't plan to address included: rehabilitation centers, inter-cousin rivalries, and not-quite breakups with not-quite boyfriends. Topics my friends had not yet addressed, but no doubt would, included: Paul.

"Glad to hear you've accomplished so much," said Marie.

"Did I ever tell you guys that I once ran into Melody at a yoga studio in the Marina?" asked Andrea.

"Yes," we said. "You've told us."

"You think she'd have a private yoga instructor come right to the house." Andrea had told us that, too.

"My cousin Suzanne just started working for Melody," said Jenny. I asked what she did.

"Some kind of assistant."

We drained our beers and pondered what life would be like as Melody's assistant.

Then Marie asked, "What's Singapore like anyway?"

"Clean," I said, lifting my elbows off the sticky table.

"Because they don't let you chew gum," said Jenny.

"And they flog you for littering," said Andrea.

A waitress brought us refills, and I raised my mug to my friends — these girls who'd left quiet, suburban towns to embark on lives that made their parents shake their heads in wonder.

"Here's to dirty, smelly, wonderful San Francisco," I said.

"Cheers," they chorused. "Welcome home."

Back at my hotel, I checked my messages — still no response. It wasn't like Paul to not write back. I thought about resending the email, but decided to give him another day. In the meantime, I looked up the phone number for my favorite restaurant.

Located in Berkeley, not far from campus, Café Mirabelle was French-inspired and wildly expensive. This was the place where Paul had proposed after making a one-night exception to his own ban on fine dining. We were twenty-four and dressed as if attending a college formal, even though other diners wore khakis and jeans. Gazing in Paul's eyes across our steak au poivre and salmon en papillote, I'd felt impossibly grown up. A few years later, we returned to Mirabelle when my parents were in town. I'd just gotten into graduate school at the conservatory, and a prestigious journal had accepted Paul's paper for publication. I squeezed my husband's hand, marveling at our incredible good fortune.

Now I dialed the restaurant's number, and when a smooth female voice answered, I made a reservation for two, hesitating for only a split second when I was asked to leave a credit card number to guarantee the table.

Outside my hotel window, the Bay Bridge gleamed through the

evening mist. The wind had picked up, and beneath the deck the black waters churned and frothed.

This dreary weather continued for the next four days as I awoke each morning to put on one of my two business suits, and traveled from my downtown hotel to the nearby convention hall, where four hundred and sixty-eight natural-foods businesses from around the world vied for the attention of American consumers. I found myself surrounded by vendors of Indian teas, Chinese ginseng, aged vinegars, fruit-infused olive oils, and other exotic foodstuffs. The woman at the neighboring table turned out to be the largest supplier of white truffle products in all of Western Europe.

The hall was overheated; the fluorescent lights were blinding; my lips ached from smiling. But when the owners of a prominent Asian supermarket chain took a taste of our premium light soy sauce and proclaimed it better than any of the ones they currently stocked, I knew I could make this trip worthwhile. I reached out to anyone who so much as slowed down in front of my table; I perfected my pitch. The proprietor of one of San Francisco's most highly regarded haute-vegetarian restaurants promised to send in his order as soon as he got back to the office. A famous chocolatier made plans to create a chocolate flavored with our dark soy sauce. By the end of the day I'd handed out most of my business cards and had to ask Shuting to Fed Ex more sauce.

Each evening I emailed my uncle a daily report, and as I detailed the interest in our company's premium soy sauce, I kept my tone neutral and did not gloat. I understood that a couple of orders here and there were hardly enough to affect Lin's long-term goals, no matter how noteworthy the buyers. It would take something much larger to convince Uncle Robert that our premium sauces could be as marketable in America as our fiberglass sauce.

Knowing that my updates would get back to Ba, I made a point of mentioning how pleased I was to be back in the city, how much I was enjoying catching up with old friends. In reality, I spent my nights alone at the hotel, looking over my notes, bracing for the onslaught of the next day. I didn't make plans to see my classmates again, and they didn't call either, aside from Jenny who sent a short, somewhat cryptic text message: *Cousin might be at trade show. Looks like me with longer hair. Say hi!*

I called home one time, the day Ma left the rehab center.

"How is she?" I asked Ba.

"She's right here," he said, and I could hear his pleasure. "Ask her yourself, *lah*."

But I stopped him before he could pass the phone. "I just wanted to check in. I don't actually have time to chat." I didn't know what was holding me back.

I heard him tell Ma, "She can't talk now." He returned to the phone. "Everything good over there?"

"Fantastic," I said.

By the fourth and final day of the show, the atmosphere in the convention hall had relaxed. A third of the vendors had already packed up and gone home. Ties discarded, heels kicked off, the remaining vendors sat around snacking on leftover samples, and I joined in, nibbling on raw sheep's milk cheese and dark chocolate seasoned with lavender sea salt.

In the middle of the afternoon, a trio of neatly dressed young women entered the hall. They paused by the large poster that mapped out vendor locations and jotted down notes on clipboards. Even though they looked too young and fashionable to be buyers, their efficient, self-assured mannerisms spurred us vendors to tidy our tables and pay attention.

Word spread quickly: the girls were not buyers, but production assistants. Production assistants for Melody. They were here to find gift ideas for the talk show host to present on air in her annual Christmas episode.

"You know who that is, right?" the white truffle supplier whisper-screamed in my ear.

At that very moment, one of the girls was walking down my aisle, studying the placard on each table. She wore tortoiseshell glasses and her straight, brown hair was pushed back with a slim headband. Every now and then she stopped to ask a question, take a sip from a thimble-sized cup, spear a toothpick in a jar.

The girl would have walked right past my table if I hadn't cried out in a shaky voice, "Susan? Is that your name by any chance?"

Startled, the girl stopped. "It's Suzanne," she said slowly. "Suzanne Silver. Have we met?"

I explained I was a friend of her cousin's and added, "Please, you must try our soy sauce."

I launched into the pitch I'd been giving all week. I was Gretchen Lin, the granddaughter of the founder of Lin's Soy Sauce. The last remaining all-natural brewer in Singapore, Lin's was on a quest to urge home chefs to replace plain old table salt with premium soy sauce. I showed her photographs of the factory and walked her through our sauce's aging process, taking time to describe Ahkong's proprietary clay jars.

The girl wrote on her clipboard and gingerly dipped a cracker in the small bowl I held out. She picked up a bottle of dark soy sauce, examined its white rice-paper wrapping, and ran her thumb over the gold sticker embossed with the Chinese character for our family name.

I took the bottle from her hands and turned it to display the writing printed on the rice paper. "*Xian chi ʐai tan,*" or "Eat first, talk later," had been my grandmother's catch phrase, delivered sternly when business discussions threatened to upstage a meal at her dining table.

Setting down her clipboard, the girl asked more questions about my family: How did your grandfather form the idea for this company? When did your uncle and father take over? How old were you when you knew you wanted to join the family business?

"Six," I lied. "I was six years old when I knew for sure."

She wrote this down.

I described Ba's dream of making soy sauce a staple for Western cooks. "He makes a stellar *boeuf bourguignon* with light soy sauce in place of salt," I told the girl. The delicate flavors of our sauce enhanced the rich *umami* taste of the meat. Our sauce rounded out the stock, highlighting the bright, acidic tomatoes, preventing the red wine from overwhelming the dish.

I told her how Ba never left the house without a sample-sized bottle of Lin's in his breast pocket, which he poured on any food placed before him, and pressed on curious bystanders.

I was afraid I'd gone on for too long, and was relieved that this little story made Suzanne Silver smile.

"Listen," she said. "I love the history and the anecdotes behind this sauce. It's exactly what we're looking for." She dug around in her leather satchel and whisked out a business card, and even though I knew whom she worked for, seeing the words printed on that square of cardstock made me want to do cartwheels up and down the aisle.

Suzanne Silver explained that Melody's Christmas episode was the most popular one of the season. "It's a wonderful opportunity, especially for less established businesses," she said, as if I didn't already know what this publicity could do for Lin's and our premium sauces.

I handed over a business card of my own — my last one — and packed up bottles of our light and dark sauces for Suzanne Silver to take back to Melody.

She waved a hand over the row of bottles on the table. "Melody would love all this," she said. "The battle between art and commerce, tradition and innovation." Her eyes lit up. "Oh, that's good." She wrote this down, too.

I tried to share more details about our factory and our production process — anything she could possibly want to know — but she smiled kindly and said she thought she had enough for now. Before she left, she said, "So, how do you know Jenny?"

I told her Jenny and I were classmates at the conservatory.

Suzanne Silver slid the clipboard in the front pocket of her leather satchel. "Jenny's still in school. So you graduated?"

I kept my words vague. "Actually, I do this now," I said as I straightened a bottle that was out of line.

The girl seemed satisfied with my answer. She promised to call if she had any news and clicked swiftly out of the hall on high-heeled pumps. As I watched her disappear through the double doors, I imagined the looks on my cousin's and uncle's faces if I managed to pull this off. And then I pictured Ma's reaction. "*Aiyah*, why are they always whining and sniveling on that show?" she'd say, refusing to admit her affection for Melody. "Good work, ducky."

The day after the trade show closed, I'd planned to continue my apartment search. Instead, with the rain showing no sign of ceasing, I sat in my hotel room, reading everything I could find about Melody, compiling a list of all the products she'd recommended in the past decade: hand-poured paraffin-wax candles from France, ultralight premium down jackets, Hawaiian organic raw honey. Once an hour, I checked my email to see if Paul had written back. Only one new email arrived—from James—a mass email addressed to probably his entire list of contacts, notifying us of the upcoming soft opening of Spice Alley restaurant. Twice I called the number on Suzanne Silver's business card to see if she needed any more information about Lin's, but she never answered the phone.

On the penultimate day of my trip, I left the hotel to meet a particularly persistent realtor in the Mission, and emerged from the underground BART station into a stream of watery sunlight that had somehow broken through the clouds. All around me, Latina mothers cried out in Spanish to chubby toddlers, old bearded men argued over chessboards, and hipsters in tight pants hurried to jobs that began in the middle of the day.

As I stood there in the center of the plaza with my chin raised to the sky, the clouds parted, revealing the full face of the sun. All at once, the wind died down, the air grew warm as an embrace. I yanked my sweater over my head, plunged a hand in my bag, plucked out my cell phone, and called Paul.

• • •

Back at the hotel, I showered, shaved, blow-dried, curled, tweezed, powdered and smoothed on a black jersey dress which, at the last minute, I'd tucked between the dark trousers and suit jackets as my father had looked on, his face betraying nothing.

Earlier on the phone, Paul didn't explain why he'd never responded to my email, saying only that he'd love to see me. I felt foolish revealing the reservation I'd made, and sure enough, when I blurted out the restaurant's name, he seemed to hesitate.

"What's the matter?" I asked in the lightest tone I could muster. "You need permission to leave the house?"

The silence continued on the other end. Then he said, "Actually, she's not here right now."

I wasn't sure what he meant, and I wasn't about to ask.

"She's been staying with a friend. She needs to be closer to campus."

A knot loosened in my chest. I didn't need more details.

I left the hotel early — traffic on the Bay Bridge was unpredictable — and pulled into a parking lot with ten minutes to spare. Sitting in my rental car, I watched couples stream out of Andronico's with reusable grocery sacks and insulated wine totes. Two kids in Cal sweatshirts got in the neighboring car and proceeded to make out for a full three minutes. At first I averted my eyes, not wanting them to catch me staring, but when it grew clear that I'd have to pound on the window and yell before they'd pay any attention to me, I watched how the boy inhaled the girl's mouth into his own, how his hands moved over her, reading the curves of her body like Braille.

After a while, the boy turned on the ignition, placed a hand on the passenger-side headrest, and began to back out. Before returning his hand to the steering wheel he ruffled the girl's hair, and that casual gesture filled me with more longing than anything else I'd witnessed.

It was two minutes to seven, time to go inside.

I emerged from the car, smoothed the wrinkles from my dress, and when I reached for my purse, the Queen of the Night's aria burst forth from my cell phone. The number was unlisted; I knew I had to answer.

It was Suzanne Silver, sounding slightly breathless, as though she'd sprinted up a flight of stairs. Melody had loved the soy sauce and the packaging and the family history. "She wants to meet you in person, and ASAP. Can you come by the office the day after tomorrow?"

I almost said yes, but then I realized that in two days I'd be on a plane back to Singapore.

"I see," said Suzanne Silver.

I wondered how difficult it would be to change my flight.

"Let me check her calendar," she said. "Would you mind holding?"

On TV, Melody was energetic yet serene, comforting yet stern—the cool, big sister you always wished you had. In real life, she had to be different: ruthless, efficient. Wasn't that how these things worked? How many other products had made the cut? How close was Lin's to actually getting on air?

I hadn't mentioned these developments to my uncle in case nothing panned out. Even if Melody ended up choosing us, we'd still need to consider how Lin's would handle the jump in sales, and export bottles quickly enough, and channel short-term momentum into long-term interest. I paced the gravel by my car, scanning the parking lot for Paul's green Subaru. I wasn't surprised he was late.

Suzanne Silver returned to the phone. "Melody's leaving for the airport in an hour. If you come right over, you can get in the limo with her. She'll chat with you on the way there." She proceeded to give me the address to the mansion I'd driven past several times before.

"Hang on," I said. "You mean right now?"

"I mean right now."

Just then I noticed Paul's dusty red road bike chained to the rack.

"Well?" said Suzanne Silver.

"I'll be there," I heard myself say, wondering how I'd explain this to Paul, how I'd convince him to meet me later.

"Great," she said. "And for what it's worth, Melody loves the human-interest angle to your sauce. That's what gets viewers to really connect with a product. She even wanted me to ask for your father's *boeuf bourguignon* recipe so we could feature it on air."

I promised to be there as soon as I could.

Instead of getting in my car, I ducked behind a red SUV and peered through the restaurant's glass doors, and then through the row of picture windows. There he was, seated at a booth by the back window with his head bent over the menu. He'd been on time after all. The stubble on his chin was fuller than before and trimmed so that his jaw appeared more angular. He looked older, gently weathered in the way that was sexy for men. He did not glance up.

I was fingering my phone, wrestling with whether to call Suzanne Silver back, when a waitress with a perky blond ponytail appeared at Paul's side with a pitcher of ice water. As she stood over the table, pouring him a glass, he said something that made her set down the pitcher, rest a hand on his shoulder and release a big, full-bodied laugh.

The back of my neck tightened. My head began to throb. I couldn't decide whether to rush in that restaurant or to find a better place to hide. Paul had cheated on me with a college girl, and now, the best I could hope for was that he would cheat on her with me. A breeze kicked up in the parking lot, and only then did I notice I was drenched in sweat. Rubbing the goose bumps from my arms, I went to my car and got in.

When Paul answered his cell phone, I said, "Hey, I'm not going to be able to make it."

"What do you mean? I've been sitting here for ten minutes."

"I have to do something for work," I said. "Something really important."

"What?" he asked, clearly confused.

I'd never told him I'd started working at Lin's, and this wasn't the time to explain. "I'm sorry," I said, and once I got started I couldn't stop. "I'm so, so sorry."

"Hey," he said in that voice that could fold itself around me and pull me to the ground. "It's okay. These things happen."

I pressed the crown of my skull into the headrest. "Thank you," I said, and willed myself to say good-bye.

"So when can I see you?"

I twisted around in my seat, craning to peer in through the restaurant window. He sat there in that booth with his chin in his hand, his face grave.

He asked, "Are you still there?"

"Yes."

"God, I've missed you."

I closed my eyes and waited for the sting to subside. "I really have to go."

Melody lived in a rose-colored palazzo overlooking the bay. I pulled up in my rental car as her staff piled the last of the Louis Vuitton luggage into the trunk of a black stretch limousine. The palazzo's vast oak doors swung open, and a statuesque figure in a white pant-suit emerged. With the hem of her trousers brushing the ground, Melody appeared to be floating across the driveway, followed by an assistant, yet another neatly dressed young woman. As they approached me, I saw that Melody was holding her cell phone to one ear. She told me to give her one minute and turned away. Her assistant smiled apologetically and waved me into the limo.

For almost the entire half-hour ride to the airport, Melody spoke sternly into her phone. Even though she was clearly reprimanding whoever was on the other end of the line, her velvety voice cushioned her words. "I wouldn't let me down again, if I were you," she said, running her burgundy fingernails through those buttery blond waves.

Finally, as the limo veered off the highway for the airport exit, Melody ended the call and dropped the phone in her assistant's waiting hands. She leaned over and touched my arm. "My apologies," she said, flashing a pair of perfectly symmetrical dimples. "Let's talk. I want to hear everything."

I didn't know how much Suzanne Silver had told her. I waited for Melody to take the lead, but she only peeked down at her large, diamond-encrusted watch.

Based on my research into Melody's previous gift choices, I'd planned out exactly what to say to convince her to choose Lin's. Now, with the airport terminal approaching, I opened my mouth and began to speak as fast as I could. I told her how my grandfather had given up a successful career to create his own soy sauce, how my father and uncle had dedicated their lives to carrying on the family tradition.

"Mm-hmm," she said blandly. She'd heard this all before.

In my mind, Melody's studio audience sprung to life, clapping and whooping, gasping and swooning. These women believed Melody could change lives, and I believed, too. That's when I dropped my pitch. I told her I was thirty years old and had spent my entire life running from the family business. In fact, if not for my failed marriage and my mother's kidney failure, I never would have returned home.

Melody's eyes seared into mine. They were the color of swimming-pool water on a scorching day. "Go on," she said.

I told her I'd always viewed my father as a man who'd been trapped — trapped into preserving his own father's vision, forced to wage a noble but futile battle against modernizing the company. Now, having worked at Lin's, I realized I'd missed the point. Traditions were important — and at Lin's we took great pride in ours — but all Ahkong and Ba ever wanted was to make the best-tasting soy sauce. "How many people get to do that for a living?" I asked, my voice rising. "How many people get to create something they're truly proud of?"

The limo stopped in front of the international terminal.

Melody smiled coolly and offered me her hand. "It's always a pleasure to talk to people who are passionate about their work. Suzanne will be in touch." With that she strode in the airport, her assistant on her heels, leaving the driver to deal with the bags.

On the return trip to the city, I settled back in the limo and tried to analyze Melody's elusive reaction. I wanted to call someone — Ba or Ma, maybe Frankie — and recount the whole crazy story, but something stopped me. What if nothing came of this meeting? What if Melody had already dismissed me, and I never heard from Suzanne? I was so caught up in the moment that I didn't pause to think about what I'd said to the talk show host, the questions I'd answered, the decisions I'd made. There was so much I couldn't acknowledge to myself, much less share with my family.

That night, I couldn't sleep. I lay with the pillow over my face, then sat up in the darkness, then paced the strip of moonlit carpet by the window. More than once I thought about calling Paul, and yet, each time, my fingers stalled over the keys.

Looking back, I'd like to be able to say that this was my moment of recognition, that what had eluded me in the limousine grew clear, and there in that darkened hotel room, I finally knew what I wanted. In truth that knowledge didn't come until morning. That night, I thought only of the waitress, her high blond ponytail and easy smile.

Late the following morning, almost afternoon, I awoke to discover I'd slept more soundly than I had in weeks, and knew it was time to go home.

At the Office of Student Services at the San Francisco Conservatory, I explained to the girl at the counter that I needed a refund of the deposit my father had paid several weeks earlier.

She accessed my file on the computer, bit her lip as she scanned the screen, and told me I couldn't take another semester off without withdrawing altogether. "Sometimes they make exceptions," she said, snapping her gum. "You know, for special cases?" She studied my face, trying to figure out if I qualified. "Want the phone number?"

I shook my head.

"Fine. The money will be credited to the original account within seven-to-ten business days." She slid over a withdrawal form and showed me where to sign.

In my pocket was the crumpled sheet of hotel notepad paper on which I'd made up a to-do list. Earlier that morning, I'd canceled my last apartment viewing, and now, upon signing my name with a flourish, I'd quit school. My only remaining task was to make a few phone calls before I boarded my plane.

I stepped out onto the sidewalk as my bus hurtled past. Instead of chasing it down, I crossed the street to the practice rooms. My ID card no longer worked, but the security guard assumed it was a problem with the magnetic strip and held open the door.

Downstairs, I heaved my shoulder into the thick, soundproof door of the small basement auditorium and the familiar musty smell of ancient velvet drapery washed over me. I switched on the lights and hoisted myself on stage.

Seated at the grand piano, I adjusted the height of the bench and flipped up the once-glossy black cover. With my hands poised dramatically over the keys, I searched my mind for a piece suitable for the finale of my life in San Francisco. After attempting a flashy

Rachmaninoff prelude I'd never truly memorized, my fingers found the Debussy piece I'd watched my mother play so many times over the past month.

I was about a third of the way through, willing the melody to pour through me, swaying my body in time, when my fingers stopped. I started and stalled, started again and lost my spot. Gazing out into the darkness, I questioned what I was doing here, why I was trying to stage this theatrical good-bye. Then my laughter rolled out of me, filling the empty hall. I'd never been a performer. I'd never even wanted to teach music. This city had been good to me, and I would miss it, but there was no need to try to feel things I didn't feel.

On my way out I waved at the security guard.

"Leaving so soon?" he asked.

"See you later," I said automatically, even though it wasn't true.

By now it was late afternoon, and the slanting pre-fall light cast long sharp shadows on the sidewalk. Back in Singapore, it was dawn of the following day. Children with backpacks waited for school buses, the elderly practiced *tai chi* in public parks, and the sun began its slow, inexorable climb.

In the airport lounge, I tackled the last item on my to-do list. I called Paul.

"I don't know how else to say this," I said. "I got in touch with a divorce attorney. You should hear from her soon."

"Wait," he said, sounding genuinely shocked. "We need to talk about this."

For the first time in my life, I felt sorry for him.

"Stay," he said.

And, "What about what I want?"

And, "It'll be different this time."

I said, "Paul, I don't live here anymore."

"Of course you do. You love it here."

I wished he would actually listen to me. "We're not kids any-more. We don't just go around doing whatever we want."

His laugh exploded in my ear. "You're telling me this?" he said. "Seriously. You are telling me this."

Anger spiked within me. But then it struck me that he'd been right all along. I had lacked focus and ambition. I'd spent all my time in San Francisco trying out jobs and earning more degrees, unable to commit to a career because the only thing I'd ever wanted was to be with him.

"You're absolutely right," I said. "You said it first, and now I'm finally taking your advice." I said good-bye, gathered my bags and walked to the gate.

Safely onboard the plane, I finally let myself consider the future awaiting me back home. My father would be thrilled by my deci-sion, but what about Ma? She'd opened up the world for me—a world she would now watch me fold up neatly and set aside. I had to make her understand that by freeing me from the family business, she'd taught me that I could do anything I chose. And now, I was choosing soy sauce.

The plane lifted into the sky. The purser advised us all to sit back, relax and enjoy the flight, and I closed my eyes, determined to try.

15

IT WAS MIDNIGHT IN SINGAPORE by the time my cherry-red suitcase sailed toward me on the conveyor belt. Sixteen hours had passed since I'd boarded the plane in San Francisco. My clothes were rumpled, my eyes red and scratchy, my hair greasy enough to wring out like a towel. Changi Airport's vast high-ceilinged baggage hall, with its polished surfaces and spotless floors, only underscored my raggedness.

Earlier, at immigration, I'd gone through the citizens-only line, flattening my passport on the scanner while visitors waited in long queues. A machine authenticated my passport, and "Welcome home" flashed on the screen in our four national languages, English, Chinese, Tamil, and Malay. I wondered if any other phrase could ever be so fraught.

Despite my fatigue, I moved swiftly through the "Nothing to Declare" lane and past the clumps of people in the waiting area. It was still hard to believe I didn't know the next time I'd be back in this airport—this place that had once been my portal to the real world, but was now a gate about to close.

I was so focused on getting a taxi that I strode right past my mother, leaning on a pillar with her hands in her pockets.

"Where are you rushing off to?" she called after me.

I pivoted on the balls of my feet, dragging my suitcase behind me. Ma's lips bore no trace of her trademark red lipstick. In fact, she wore no makeup at all. A loose linen tunic and matching trousers hung off her slight frame. What would have looked like pajamas on anyone else, on her appeared elegant, effortless.

"What are you doing here?" I asked. "Did you come alone? Does Ba know?"

She brushed away my concerns. "You think I climbed out the window while he was asleep?"

We rode the escalator down to the parking lot, and she yanked the carry-on tote from my arm, even though I told her, several times, that I could manage on my own. When we got to the car, she insisted I take the wheel since she couldn't see that well at night.

"Exactly," I said. "You shouldn't be driving. I could have easily taken a cab."

"Is it so bizarre for me to meet my daughter at the airport? I want to hear about your trip."

I didn't know where to begin, so I adjusted the mirrors, started the car and turned up the radio. To the strains of Eric Clapton's *Tears in Heaven*, we drove out of the parking lot and onto the wide boulevard lined with orange and fuchsia bougainvilleas—a sight so familiar and so distinctly local, it filled me with warmth, no matter how many times I took this road.

"I've always hated his voice. Too whiny." Ma turned off the radio. "So?" she said.

I'd hoped to have time to digest the events of the past week and prepare what I wanted to say, but Ma was ready to talk now. When I saw the neon sign of a twenty-four-hour hawker center, I swerved into the entrance.

Inside the hawker center, we chose a table at a coffee stall overlooking the beach, as far away as possible from a gaggle of middle-aged *tai tais* who had just concluded a late-night mahjong session and were recapping its highlights. Ma and I took long sweet sips of our *kopi-pos,* weak coffee with a generous dollop of condensed milk. The breeze off the water was brisk and alive.

I inhaled sharply and began. I told Ma about the trade show and how good it felt to represent the family business; about how proud I thought Ba would be of all the contacts I'd made and the groundwork I'd laid in the US market, and how I hoped she could be proud of me, too. I explained why I didn't think Lin's would survive under Cal, and why the company had to revamp its US strategy, and I told her about meeting Melody — Yes! *The* Melody! — though probably nothing would come of it.

Ma looked bewildered, but I didn't slow down because there was so much more to say. It was time to reveal that I'd begun divorce proceedings and withdrawn from school. The words were surprisingly difficult to get out. Even now, I couldn't shut off the part of me that longed to please my mother. "I've made up my mind," I said. "I'm staying here, in Singapore, for good."

She tried to interject, but I kept going. "I'm sorry to disappoint you. I'm sorry you think I'm throwing everything away. But I don't want the things you want."

"Why would I be disappointed?" Ma asked quietly.

"All you've ever wanted is for Paul and me to live happily ever af-ter in America—for us to have what you never had." I'd already said too much, but I couldn't stop. "You need to accept that I'm not you."

The mahjong ladies pretended not to eavesdrop.

Ma's lower lip trembled. "I'm sorry you feel this way."

I stared back at her, puzzled and exasperated. It wasn't like her not to fight back.

She reached for her coffee mug, but her hands shook so badly, she placed it back on the table. She said, "All I've ever wanted is for you to be able to do whatever you want." Beneath the fluorescent lights, her bare face looked tired, worn.

"I want this, Ma. I want to work at Lin's. I want to make soy sauce. I want to be here with you and Ba and the rest of my family."

Out on the beach, a wave broke on the shore with a deafening crash. In the heart of the city, where we spent most of our time, it was easy to forget we were surrounded by water. A second wave crested, and I pictured it continuing to rise, coming right for my mother and me. Was she bracing herself? Holding her breath?

Again Ma reached for the mug, this time managing to take a small sip. She said, "So, you're getting a divorce."

All my anger and self-righteousness surged back through me. "This may come as a shock to you, but your son-in-law left me. I begged him to stay, but he went off to live with his girlfriend. His twenty-one-year old girlfriend."

Across the table Ma looked sad—sad and weary—not at all fu-rious like I expected, and certainly not shocked.

"He cheated on me, Ma."

Ma's eyelids fell, and when her eyes blinked open they brimmed with tears. "I know, ducky," she said, pressing her hands to mine. "I know."

I was sobbing so hard I didn't even question how she'd known, who had told her. A moment later, she was wrapping her thin arms around me, rocking me gently from side to side.

By now, the only other person within hearing distance was the old man behind the counter who politely occupied himself with re-arranging plastic cups and plates. I wondered if he could see us for who we were: a pair of women, trying to take care of themselves and each other, falling short time and again.

When I calmed down, I considered Ma's reaction. Where was the anger and outrage? Why hadn't she told me she'd found out about the affair?

Ma lowered her head. "Maybe this was wrong of me," she said slowly, a rare admission. "But I wanted you to see him." At first, she said, she'd wanted me to go back to America to reclaim my life, and then, when Frankie told her what Paul had done, she'd wanted me to confront my choices. The last thing she wanted was for me to retreat into permanent hiding in Singapore.

"Is that what you think I'm doing?"

Her fingers combed through my hair, massaging my scalp. "No."

"Is that what you think you did?"

She gazed up at the ceiling fan, spinning so sluggishly you could see a layer of dust on each blade. Her hands formed two small fists. "When I first came home, I was irate. I thought I could have been a brilliant scholar at a top American university, and instead I was trapped in a classroom of students whose marks were too low to study anything but literature."

"I see why that was difficult."

Ma shook her head. "Maybe at first, but over time, these obstacles became excuses. I could have pushed harder. I could have finished my manuscript." She pressed her fingertips to the corners of her eyes, and gave a wry laugh. "If I'd stayed in the US, I would have ended up at a small college in a small town, equally convinced that my talent was going to waste."

"And you wouldn't have Ba."

She took another sip from her mug. "That's right."

Outside, the sky was growing light, painting the world in hues of pale gray, and the birds had begun to rise. The ocean had receded and now lapped gently at the sand.

"You're not me. I know that," she said. "You're going to be brilliant at Lin's, and I'm sorry I ever stood in your way."

"Brilliant is a strong word. I think I'll do well."

She stroked my hair. "My girl, my only child. It's good to have you here."

Together we squinted into the distance. Dawn in Singapore was afternoon in San Francisco. It would take my mind a while to stop trying to exist in two places, but I was ready.

I didn't fault Frankie for telling my mother about Paul.

At work the next day, I pulled her into my office and shut the door. "Frankie, you don't have to explain. I understand where you were coming from." I expected relief, but saw only confusion.

"Really? You're sure?"

I told her she'd done me a favor: I'd kept the affair from my mother for far too long, and Frankie had given me a much-needed push. In fact, Ma and I had sorted it all out the night before. "Can you tell I hardly slept?" I rubbed my eyes.

She gave me a worried smile, and I patted her arm. "Paul and I are done. I'm here to stay."

Far from being happy for me, Frankie slumped forward in her chair and buried her face in her hands.

"Wait," I said. "I thought you hated him."

"I hooked up with James." She squeezed shut her eyes as if bracing for an explosion.

The muscles in my face went slack. I could feel my smile melt away. "Oh," I said. "That I didn't know."

Then it was her turn to reach for my arm. "I'm sorry, I really am. It was one time."

I pulled away. I sat very still and tried to decide how I felt, but the only thing I could think about was how much I wanted her to get out of that chair and leave my office.

Finally I said, "We broke up."

"I know. I'm still sorry."

I turned to my computer screen and told her I had a mountain of email to go through. She mumbled one last apology before getting up to leave.

It wasn't just an excuse. I didn't have time to fixate on whatever had happened between Frankie and James. In the week I'd been away, my father and uncle had moved no closer to a resolution. Something had to change.

16

MR. LIU WAS SEVENTEEN YEARS OLD when Ahkong hired him to be the company's first errand boy. Through the years, he worked his way up to office manager, went back to school at Ahkong's urging to earn a chemistry degree, and returned as Lin's food scientist — a post he'd held for the last thirty years. If anyone had insight into how Ahkong would have handled the current family feud, it would be him.

I found Mr. Liu in his office by the factory floor, looking through files.

He raised his head in surprise. "Come in," he said in Chinese. "What can I do for you?"

I sat down, suddenly shy. As a child, I'd spent hours in this office with a coloring book and a package of rice crackers, while he and my father took care of business elsewhere in the factory. Since my return, however, it hadn't occurred to me to ask Mr. Liu what he thought of Cal's mistake, or the fiberglass sauce, or any of the other developments at the company.

I saw no point in being coy. "I need your advice. What do you think we should do about Cal?"

Even when he frowned, Mr. Liu's narrow, lined face radiated kindness. "I can't tell you anything you don't already know. A family business is just that — a family."

I tried to parse the meaning of his words.

He said, "Remember this: no matter what your family decides, the boy will remain in your life. He's not going to disappear. He will always be your cousin, and your father's nephew, and your uncle's son."

Something clicked into place. Of course Mr. Liu was the one who'd notified my father when Cal arrived for the Mama Poon meeting.

"I should have come to you sooner," I said.

His eyes disappeared when he smiled. "You came at the right time."

An hour later, I left Mr. Liu's office and went to find my father. "Govern a family as you would cook a small fish — very gently." I said, repeating the Chinese proverb Mr. Liu had told me.

Ba set down his pen. "Your ahkong used to say that."

"You need to give Cal another chance. Lin's belongs to him as much as it is belongs to you, or Uncle Robert." After a pause I added, "Or me." Seventy-two hours had passed since I'd announced my decision to stay.

Ba shook his head. "I already told you I don't trust him."

In Chinese, I said, "One cannot refuse to eat just because there is a chance of being choked."

228

"I see you've been talking to Mr. Liu." He gave me a tight-lipped smile.

I admitted I didn't necessarily trust Cal either, but I also believed he wouldn't dare behave so recklessly this time around, not with so many people watching him. In the end, he, too, wanted Lin's to thrive.

Ba wrapped one hand in the other and cracked his knuckles.

"Must you do that?" I asked.

He dropped his hands. "What kind of message would it send if I let Cal come back?"

"That you believe that being a Lin makes you uniquely suited to running this company."

He said, "The boy has already proven he cares more about money than soy sauce."

"You and Uncle Robert don't agree on everything, and yet you've worked together for years. There might be hope for Cal and me."

Ba pointed his index finger at me. "You think you can do this. You think you can work with him."

I said I wasn't sure, but I also knew I had no choice.

My father held my gaze as he lifted the telephone to his ear. "*Di-ah,*" he said into the mouthpiece. Younger brother. "I'm with Xiao Xi. Come over. And bring the boy."

Later that afternoon, the four of us emerged from Ba's office and headed to the conference room, where the entire company had assembled for an important announcement. I quickened my pace to keep up with my father and uncle, but Cal took me by the elbow. "Gretch, I wanted to say thank you."

I'd never expected to hear those words from Cal. But then again,

I'd spent so little time in Singapore these past years, I hardly knew the adult him. People changed with age; they outgrew their stubbornness and volatility.

I said, "I'm really looking forward to working with you."

Cal's mouth twisted in a half smile. "You just saved the venerable Lin's Soy Sauce from going bust."

It was a joke—an inappropriate joke, and I told myself to let it go.

As Cal and I made our way to the front of the conference room, where our fathers stood, I studied the scuffed tips of my shoes, ignoring the weight of my co-workers' gazes.

Uncle Robert thanked everyone for gathering here. "Effective immediately," he said, "Cal and Gretchen will be Lin's co–vice presidents."

Around the room, heads turned, eyebrows raised, eyes met. In one corner, Shuting smiled smugly at Fiona, as if this were the outcome she'd predicted all along. On the opposite side of the room, one sales guy whispered to another as they shot sidelong glances my way.

My uncle went on: Cal would continue to oversee the Mama Poon deal, which was progressing so smoothly the launch date had been moved up to early March. I, on the other hand, would manage the premium line, which from now on would be known as the *heritage* line. Thanks to my success at the trade show in San Francisco, our premium sauces would soon be exported to the United States, albeit in small quantities.

Beside me, my cousin beamed. He folded his fingers into a pistol and pretended to fire at someone across the room. That our responsibilities were far from equal was clear to him and me and the entire company. His project was Lin's largest and potentially most profitable growth opportunity. Mine carried mostly symbolic importance.

Finally, Uncle Robert wrapped up his announcement. "Lin's can indeed have the best of both worlds," he cried, taking his son's hand and thrusting it in the air like they were a pair of Olympic medalists. "Here's to the future."

The room burst into applause.

Uncle Robert shook my hand in a manner that was surprisingly formal. "Welcome to the team."

"Congrats, partner," Cal said, holding out his palm for me to give him five.

I put aside my animosity and slapped his palm. "Congrats."

My father gave me a big hug and said in a low voice, "So far, so good." My mother was doing well at home, and he looked better rested than he had in weeks. Later, when Ma asked what had made him change his mind about Cal, Ba would wink at me and say, "We all make sacrifices for the people we love."

At the opposite end of the conference room, Frankie stood apart from everyone else with her back against the wall, her face shielded by that curtain of hair. Though she'd tried several times to talk to me since her confession, I'd managed to avoid her — no simple feat given that we passed each other in the hall a dozen times a day. Ours appeared to be another one of those female friendships doomed by attraction to the same man, and not a very worthy man at that.

Uncle Robert raised a hand and the room quieted down. He had more news — news that I'd already heard about: Frankie had received an offer from a top management consulting firm. She would leave for Hong Kong at the end of the month.

Murmurs filled the room. The same people who continued to keep their distance from me streamed over to shake Frankie's hand or give her a hug.

"Don't forget to come back and visit us, *hor*. Hong Kong isn't that far away," Uncle Robert said, wagging a finger at Frankie. "And thank you for all your hard work."

The applause started once more, and Frankie blushed. As I clapped along, an image surfaced in my mind, of the two of us in my red Jetta, driving south on 101 to LA, a half-empty bag of marshmallows between us. She was at the wheel; I was slouched in the passenger seat with my heels on the dashboard. And when the opening drum beats of our favorite Radiohead song came on the radio, we threw back our heads and belted out the words.

That same day, Mama Poon soft-launched our soy sauce in their California stores, and Benji Rosenthal wrote to congratulate Lin's on the enthusiastic response from customers. He had his analysts reforecast sales, and they put in a request for more bottles as soon as they could get them.

Cal reported this news at the management team's midweek meeting. The four of us, plus the heads of marketing and finance, were gathered in my uncle's office.

"Excellent news, Boy," said Uncle Robert.

Cal sat up straight in his chair, as though his sternum were attached to the ceiling by a piece of string.

"I'll get someone started on the press release right away," said the marketing head.

"Nice work," I said to my cousin, who grinned back and said, "Any news to report from the premium line? Excuse me, the *heritage* line?"

I looked down at my notes, pretending I hadn't memorized what I was about to share. I told them I too had exciting news. In fact, I'd received confirmation that very morning. From the famous American talk show host herself.

Everyone leaned in. The smirk slid off my cousin's face.

"Come December, our premium soy sauce will be featured in Melody's Christmas episode as one of six gifting ideas for the season." Fighting to maintain a steady tone, I recounted the entire story, from my initial conversation with Suzanne Silver to my meeting with the talk show host in the back of her limo. "They've already ordered eight hundred bottles each of premium light and dark soy sauce to hand out to the audience and crew."

At first no one said anything.

Ba planted a hand on my shoulder and squeezed.

Then my uncle repeated Melody's name. "Incredible," he said.

The head of finance tapped numbers into his calculator. "We'll need to do some research to figure out the potential lift in sales. This could drive up numbers in a way we've never seen before."

"We'll have to notify the local news outlets," said the head of marketing, scribbling in her notebook. "This is Melody we're talking about."

But Cal reminded everyone not to get overexcited. He said the finance head was right; more research needed to be done. "We don't know how long this interest will last, and how many additional bottles we'll actually sell."

I resisted the urge to tell him to stop being a sore loser. He knew this was a once-in-a-lifetime opportunity. There was no better time to export our premium soy sauce to America.

It didn't take long for Uncle Robert and Ba to conclude that at the very least, we would have to revisit the US expansion plan.

"We need to hold off on producing more fiberglass sauce for Mama Poon's," Uncle Robert said. "At least until we have a better idea of what this publicity will do for our heritage line."

The rest of us nodded in agreement—all except for Cal who sat completely still. "Hang on. We can't afford to wait on this."

Uncle Robert began to respond, but Cal cut him off. "Why are we all rushing to make sauce the old way? Liter for liter, the fiberglass sauce is going to be twice as profitable."

This time Ba spoke. "We're not rushing into anything. That's the point, what. We need to see more analysis before we make a decision."

Cal slammed a palm on the desk. "This is our problem. We're too damn slow about everything. By the time we make up our minds, the opportunity is gone."

"Boy," Uncle Robert said in a voice I'd never heard before. He did not go on.

"This is bullshit," Cal said, leaning forward in his chair. "It's bad enough, this 'co–vice president' crap." He glared at me.

The marketing and finance heads shifted uneasily and regarded their laps.

Cal said, "Am I the only one who sees that Lin's can't survive this way?"

Suddenly I was furious at myself for letting him bully me. I said, "You can't throw a tantrum every time things don't go your way. There are two of us now, so yes, it's going to take a little more time to make decisions, but surely you've learned how dangerous your recklessness can be."

Cal's eyes narrowed. He rose to his feet. "Do you know how many job offers I'm sitting on? I don't have to stick around here, fighting to drag this company into the future." He stared at my uncle, as though willing—or begging—his father to back him up.

Uncle Robert's face was soft and sad. He looked away and closed his eyes.

Cal pointed right at me. His finger didn't waver as he moved to the door. "She can't handle this. Lin's is never going to make it."

The door slammed. A pile of papers flew off the desk, and I fell to my knees to gather them, relieved to have something to do.

By lunchtime, Cal was gone. He'd barged in Frankie's office and taken as many boxes of documents as he could carry, as well as a hard drive's worth of confidential files—information that had never left the family.

"We'll take him to court," I said.

But Ba said things were more complicated than that. He told me to think of what the media coverage would do to the family, especially Auntie Tina. Ba and I both turned to my uncle, who had yet to say a word.

Uncle Robert let out a rueful laugh that gave me chills. He said, "How could I be so wrong?"

"He took the files in a fit of anger. We don't know that he's planning to do anything with them," my father said. "You should talk to the boy."

But my uncle turned his back to us. "What good would that do?"

"Maybe I should talk to him," I said, even though I had no idea where to begin, even though I was the reason Cal had stormed out in the first place.

"It's worth a try," said Ba.

Uncle Robert flung his hands in the air. "Be my guest," he said, with that same bone-chilling laugh. "Be my guest."

17

IN THE WEEKS AFTER LEAVING San Francisco, I only heard
from Paul once, the day he received the papers from my lawyer.
I let the call go to voicemail, and then listened to the message
three times in a row.

Haltingly, Paul said he would mail the papers back to me later
that day. After a long pause, he said he wanted me to know that he'd
moved into a studio in Oakland, and then immediately added, "I
have no idea why I just told you that." I almost smiled.

When the honey-colored manila envelope bearing his elongated,
all-caps handwriting arrived at my parents' home, I should have
been prepared. Still, I thumbed through the stack of papers, searching for errors, a small part of me hoping for a reason to send them
back, to delay the process for a little bit longer. But all fourteen
pages had been signed and dated.

Paul and I had neither babies, nor pets, nor shared assets. We lived
eight thousand miles apart. We were young. Later, people would tell

me how lucky I was. How simple this all had been. They'd go on to recount traumatic divorces involving shell-shocked children and drained bank accounts. Paul and I should be thankful to have been spared this next level of heartbreak. With these papers, it was as if the last twelve years had never happened, or at least ceased to matter. A clean break.

Between the last two pages, my fingers sensed a thickness. I drew out a thin white envelope, unsealed but with the flap tucked in. Paul's final plea? He'd always had a melodramatic streak.

I fumbled with the flap before ripping open the envelope. It was not a letter, but a check, made out to my father, for two thousand seven hundred dollars, and a short note detailing Paul's plan to pay off the rest of the money. In spite of it all, my heart lurched.

The sounds of plunking piano keys lugged me away from my thoughts. Downstairs, my mother was practicing dutifully. Only she could play this piece so tentatively yet with such determination.

And then my thoughts shaped themselves around the present moment: Were these small, daily activities—practicing piano, reading, working on her manuscript—enough to keep her occupied? Enough to make her days and months and years add up to something?

The day before, my mother had told me that friends of hers were looking to rent out the condo their oldest son had vacated for a larger place. "Twelve hundred square feet, two bedroom two bath." Would I be interested in taking a look?

With all that had taken place over the past weeks, I hadn't had time to consider moving out of my parents' house. And then I grasped the other reason why the thought had never crossed my mind. "If it's okay with you and Ba, I'd like to stay here for a little while."

Ma's head jerked toward me. Her eyes widened. "Of course, ducky," she said. "Stay as long as you'd like."

Downstairs, the plunking continued. My metronome had done nothing for her. In all likelihood she'd chucked it in the piano bench and forgotten about it. I could hear her now: "If I'd known you were going to nag me all day long, I would never have signed up for lessons."

I put aside the papers and went downstairs to intervene.

18

AND SO, ONCE AGAIN, I found myself at the gates of the Tan home.

Judging from the line of cars stretching down the road, Kat had managed to round up the whole group despite the short notice. I wasn't surprised.

A few days before, I'd called to apologize for my earlier behavior, and to update her on the events of the past weeks — I wanted her to hear it all from me.

Kat congratulated me on my decision to stay and dismissed my apology. That dinner had happened so long ago, she pointed out, and in our twenty-four-year friendship, hadn't we been through worse?

I wasn't sure we had, but I agreed, relieved to have my friend back.

"Now," Kat said, "I don't want to upset you, but I'm hosting a going-away party. For Frankie."

Before I could launch into my tirade, she went on. "Look, she did a shitty thing. I'm not trying to argue otherwise."

"In that case, since we're both in agreement here, why are you throwing this party? How can you do this to me?"

"She's really sorry, Gretch. Trust me."

Of course I knew how close Kat and Frankie were. Over the past months they'd spent twice as much time together as I had with either of them. Still, at that moment, the thought of the two of them talking behind my back, confiding in each other, trading advice, was too much to handle. And so I raised my voice, spoke in hyperbole, cited betrayal and made other melodramatic accusations.

True to form, Kat held her ground. "For God's sake, you don't have to hug and slobber all over each other, but at least part on decent terms. Who knows when you'll see her again?"

When I didn't acquiesce, she added, "This is Singapore. Look around you. Everyone's dated everyone else. If I stopped talking to every girl who hit on one of my ex-boyfriends, I'd have no one to talk to."

"He wasn't my boyfriend," I said quickly.

"Even more reason to come."

As I walked down the driveway, laughter rose from inside the house. A vigorous masculine laugh stood out—a laugh that could have belonged to James. I'd assumed he would be here. I'd even looked forward to showing him I could be civil. Right then, however, my instincts took over. I turned and ran to the gate, and when a taxi passed I almost flagged it down.

Two houses down, the taxi came to a stop. Terrence stepped out before helping Cindy to her feet. They called my name and waved, and Cindy said they were late because she'd barely been able to fit through the front door—what was my excuse? Her cheeks were flushed and her forehead glistened, but her smile was radiant.

"I had some things to take care of," I said, as Terrence elbowed Cindy in the ribs.

"Ow," she cried, before a look of recognition passed over her. "Oh, gosh," she said, stumbling over an apology while Terrence buried his face in his hands.

A second later, she elbowed Terrence back.

"Ow," he said, which made me laugh. And then he joined in, and Cindy giggled along.

Inside the house, the atmosphere was mellow, relaxed, unlike Kat's regular parties. People curled up on the circular couch with oversized tumblers of red wine. They lounged in deck chairs by the pool. The guest of honor stood with her elbows on the bar, swigging a Tiger beer as she chatted with Kat and Ming. Her one-time fling was all the way on the other end of the room with his friend Pierre and a girl with a pixie haircut.

When I came in the door, all eyes darted to me at the same moment. I squared my shoulders and strode through the room, and a downbeat later, conversations resumed, but still I felt them watching for my next move.

Cindy was waylaid by a girl who pressed her palms to her belly as if she were blessing the unborn child. A group of guys out on the patio called for Terrence to come over and help them resolve a bet. And then I was alone.

There was no point in prolonging the inevitable. I marched over to Kat, Ming, and Frankie, and interrupted their conversation, hugging the first two before gingerly putting my arms around Frankie.

She said, "I'm glad you came."

"I wouldn't have missed it," I said, which drew an approving smile from Kat.

Kat reached for a wine glass, filled it almost to the brim with sauvignon blanc, and carefully slid it over to me. She made up an excuse to leave, and nudged her husband to join her.

I took a long, tart, too-cold drink. "Maybe we should go outside?"

Frankie and I went out by the pool, but after she slapped at a mosquito for the third time, we retreated to the kitchen, where the only other person in the room was the maid, frying samosas in a large deep pan. Together Frankie and I watched the girl shuttle her samosas from pan to paper towel to serving platter.

The maid finished stacking the samosas and offered the platter to Frankie and me. I shook my head, and was taken aback when Frankie reached for one; I'd grown accustomed to her declining most everything.

Platter in hand, the maid went out to the living room.

"I know," Frankie said, catching my look. "I shouldn't be doing this."

I denied that the thought had even occurred to me.

She attempted to bite into the samosa, then gave up and thrust the whole thing in her mouth, dropping her jaw and panting to cool the piping-hot triangle. When she finished chewing, she said glumly, "I'm so afraid that everything will go back to the way it was before."

I knew she wasn't simply referring to her weight, but I automatically started to tell her that one samosa wouldn't make a difference.

She sucked the grease off her fingers. "You don't get it. I've never been as happy as I am here in Singapore."

All at once the kitchen smells were suffocating. My stomach churned. "Frankie, you don't have to go."

"Yes, I do," she said.

"You can find another job here. I'm sure my father and uncle will help."

She balled up her napkin in her fist with surprising force. "I'm about to start a great job. I'm not going to turn it down now. And who knows? Maybe I'll love Hong Kong, too."

If I'd followed Frankie's lead and told her all I knew of Hong Kong, our conversation might have taken a lighter, more optimistic turn. Instead I made myself ask the question on my mind. "Are you leaving because of me?"

She gave me a long look. "I have to take responsibility for my actions."

"I'm not mad anymore," I said, and knew it was the truth.

Frankie's face crumpled, and I feared she'd start to cry, but then she said, "For once the guy I was attracted to actually liked me back. I know how stupid and trivial it sounds, but for me it felt monumental. I'm sorry I let that cloud my judgment. I'm sorry I hurt you."

I wanted to reach out and touch my friend's cheek. "I accept your apology."

These past months, I'd watched Frankie slip effortlessly into her new Singaporean life. She'd cultivated an uncomplicated love for my homeland, embracing her freedom and independence the way I had in America, the way I was incapable of doing here.

Now, however, I saw that I'd let my envy blind me. Nothing had been easy for Frankie. She'd had to work for everything she'd earned: the respect of my father and uncle, the trust of her co-workers, the affection of her new friends. By being courageous and persistent, she'd built the foundation for her life here in Singapore, only to have to move to Hong Kong and start over again, and all on her own, because her family had never nurtured and supported her the way mine had. Through her time here, Frankie had illuminated everything I'd given up by coming back to Singapore. Now, I finally saw what I had gained.

"I wish I could have done more to help," I said

Her brow relaxed. "You found me a job, introduced me to your family and friends — you've done more than enough."

It was kind of her to say so, but we both knew it wasn't true. I'd been petty and jealous, wrapped in the cocoon of my problems, unable to see beyond my pain.

"I should be the one thanking you," I said.

Frankie looked confused.

"If not for you, I don't think I would have given Lin's a chance. I never would have decided to stay."

She let out a honking laugh. "It's true, you were pretty awful at it in the beginning."

I playfully punched her arm. "Excuse me, Miss Fiberglass-and-Clay-What's-the-Difference-Anyway."

As we grinned at each other across the kitchen table, I knew we would never again be as close as we'd been in college. Eventually she would move on from Hong Kong to yet another new city, and our paths would cross less and less. Already I was wistful for the girls we'd once been, as someday I'd be wistful for these months we'd shared in Singapore.

At last, Frankie said, "My flight leaves at six a.m. I should probably start saying good-bye."

"I'll be first," I said, getting to my feet and hugging her tight.

"Bye, Gretch," she said, and pushed open the door.

I lingered in the kitchen, staring into my empty glass. In its watery depths I saw Frankie's mom, standing in the driveway of her squat, single-story Fresno home, receding into the distance as she waved.

When the maid returned, I was still staring at the same spot. She laid the empty platter in the sink and turned on the tap. "Still here?" she asked gently without glancing my way. "Have everything you need, nah?"

My eyes followed her quick, assured motions. I told her I did.

Outside, Frankie was moving around the living room, tearfully hugging her new friends. A dwindling plate of homemade cupcakes was being passed around. As the plate traveled toward me, someone turned and nearly smashed the remaining cupcakes, frosting first, into my chest.

"Oh, shit," said James.

"Close call," I said. An unexpected calm settled over me. I took a cupcake just to have something to do and passed on the plate.

We ate in silence, and then I said, "How've you been?"

"All right," he answered. "You?"

I saw Kat watching me from across the room. "I've been great," I said, licking the crumbs from the corners of my mouth.

"I hear you've decided to stick around."

"The rumors are true."

"For what it's worth," he said, "which is probably nothing, I'm sorry."

I turned to face him and imagined leveling those spiky tufts of hair with my palm. "For what's it worth, I think you should reevaluate your hairstyle," I said. "And I forgive you." I excused myself and went to join Kat.

"Everything okay?" she asked.

I reached an arm around her, my dear old friend who never let me get away with anything, who always took me back.

In the entranceway, Frankie stopped to slip on her shoes and gave us all a final wave. I waved back. How wondrous it felt to be one of the many staying behind.

As she disappeared around the door, her eyes met mine.

I mouthed the words, "Call when you land," and she mouthed back that she would.

After that, people began to stream out the door; it was a week-night after all.

Kat yawned languidly, and Ming laughed. "We're getting old," he said.

"It's not even midnight," someone else said, but she was yawning, too.

"Finish off that last bottle before you all leave," said Kat, bossy even through her fatigue, but this time no one listened.

"Does anyone need a ride?" James asked.

I shook my head along with the others.

When everyone had left, I helped Kat and Ming shuttle glasses and plates to the kitchen, and then I too said good-bye.

Alone outside the house, I buckled the ankle straps of my sandals.

The following day I would try, once again, to get in touch with my cousin. Since charging out of the office, he'd boycotted all family gatherings. Even Auntie Tina hadn't heard from him, and my uncle still refused to say his name. I'd sent emails, left voicemails; I'd driven to his house and banged on the door—all in an attempt to make him acknowledge what he and I both knew: that the fragrant, tawny broth my grandfather had created would always bind us together. Lin's was as much his as it was mine, and this would always be the company's greatest weakness and its greatest strength.

I knew I might fail to convince Cal to return, that by the time I got a hold of him I could be too late. But when I stopped to look beyond the surface, I saw my cousin was not so different from me: someone hell-bent on living his life one way, only to realize, years later, that he couldn't remember when and how he'd made that choice. Eventually, I might have no other option than to take him to court to save our soy sauce, and if forced to do it, I would. But I'd proceed with compassion, never downplaying the difficulties of adapting to a world that wasn't at all how you thought it would be.

In the coming days there would be factors to consider, decisions to be made. But on this night, as I walked out of my old friend's childhood home and into the warm, still air, I cleared those thoughts from my mind.

I pictured my parents awake in the darkness of their bedroom, listening for me to come in, as they had when I was a teenager. By the time I climbed the stairs, Ma would be peering out her room. "You're back," she'd say.

"I am."

"Get some sleep."

"I will."

"She's back," I'd hear her say to Ba as she closed the door, and he would reply with a grunt.

In reality, they were probably snoring softly in bed.

Beneath the streetlights of Kat's neighborhood, the empty road curved and disappeared around a bend. In surrounding houses, lamps snapped off and curtains were drawn. For now, I set one foot in front of the other, enjoying the pleasure of being alone, of having no one to hurry home to, and no place I needed to be.